THE JUDAS HOUR

Also by Howard Hunt aka "E. Howard Hunt"

Stranger in Town
Dark Encounter
The Violent Ones

as "Robert Dietrich"

The Cheat
One for the Road
Be My Victim

The Steve Bentley Thrillers

Murder on the Rocks
End of a Stripper
The House on Q Street
Mistress to Murder
Murder on Her Mind
Angel Eyes
Curtains for a Lover
Calypso Caper
Curtains for a Lover
My Body
Guilty Knowledge

THE JUDAS HOUR

HOWARD HUNT

CUTTING EDGE

ISBN-13: 978-1-952138-51-5

Published by
Cutting Edge Books
PO Box 8212
Calabasas, CA 91372
www.cuttingedgebooks.com

CHAPTER ONE

Fog brushed the grimy window and drifted back into the night, leaving droplets that trickled slowly down the soot-streaked pane. Inside the room a light was burning, the bulb hanging starkly from its own cord. Its staring brilliance sought out the dirt-filled corners, the torn carpeting, the cracked mirror, the water dripping from a bent faucet, the man lying face down on the disarrayed bed.

The room stank of forty-nine-cent wine. It stank anciently of pork and beans warmed over cans of Sterno, of unwashed bodies and vomit. It stank of stale tobacco and smoke, a smell that needed a fire to destroy it completely, and leave in its place the sterile scent of cinders and fresh ashes.

The man on the bed did not mind the fog or the stench or the light's painful brilliance. His eyes were closed and he breathed easily in relaxed, drunken rhythm. Someone had given him a pint of muscatel that afternoon, and he had brought it to the room and drunk it, mixing tap water with it to make it last longer. When the wine was finished he had thrown the bottle into the closet, where it smashed against other discarded bottles, and then he had stumbled back to the bed and closed his eyes.

Off Alcatraz a tanker hooted dismally. The muffled sound carried across San Francisco Bay, over the Embarcadero, and into the room off Market Street. Hearing it distantly, the man stirred; something in the back of his drink-dulled mind reacted to the sound of a ship making its lonely way through the fog. His right hand opened, then closed. The tanker's foghorn bleated again, but this time the man did not stir. Whatever had made him start to wake was gone now, forgotten in the depths of his stupor, lost in the vast distance of his dream.

Fog pushed its way back to the window and clung to the frame like putrid flesh.

On Lincoln Way a highly polished prewar sedan nosed through the fog, its yellow fog lamps slanting downward against the moisture-covered highway. In the glass-partitioned compartment behind the driver, four people watched the fog; the fifth, seated between two men, was asleep. The woman turned her eyes from the road and spoke to the men on the rear seat.

"How is he, Heinz?"

"Still sleeping, comrade." He spread the sleeping man's eyelids, struck a match, and waved it slowly before the unconscious eyes. The glow showed a face old and lined, covered with the white fuzz of a neglected beard.

The fourth man leaned forward, took a heavy gold watch from a vest pocket, and looked at it. "We must reach there soon," he said. "Otherwise our sleeper may wake."

The woman said, "You should have made provision for the fog, Comrade Doctor."

The doctor replaced his watch and peered out of the window. "It was incalculable, dear Nelda, and I am not in a mood to receive criticism."

A street light shone against an intersection sign. The woman said, "We are almost there." She took out a cigarette and lighted it with a flame that wavered in her shaking hand.

The doctor said, "Calm yourself. It is almost over."

"I suppose so," she said. "We've done the hardest part and got away with it."

One of the two guards laughed shortly. "It was easy," he said. "Easy. I thought it might be hard until I saw what the morning papers said. But they played it just like the doctor figured."

The doctor said, "Whatever is foreseeable I will for-see. Final success cannot derive from a series of failures."

Nelda asked, "How long must we stay here?"

"It depends partly upon yourself; partly upon the speed with which your friend can be prepared to fly." He looked at her through the darkness. "You must not lose sight of him."

She exhaled irritatedly. "He hasn't left his room for a week," she said. "The investigator gave him a bottle of wine this morning, and he passed out."

"Was it done in a manner that will not cause inquiry?"

Nelda stubbed out her cigarette. "This man gets paid too well to ask questions. Thinks I'm just a jealous wife checking up on a drunken husband."

"It is your responsibility. As you know, you are personally accountable."

"I know," she said. "I know. You don't have to worry about my part of it. My plans don't depend on the weather."

The doctor began to say something, then stopped as the car swung suddenly from Lincoln Way, passed through tall stone posterns, and began climbing a pebbled road that wound through dark trees toward a mansion on the hillside. A bronze sign said, "Private. Waverly Rest Home. Refuge From Worry, Illness, and Fear. Personal Direction of Dr. Franz Loor, Bern, Switzerland."

From the back seat the woman could hear Heinz laugh coarsely. "That's a hot one, Doc," he said. "Freedom from fear."

When Dr. Loor came downstairs, they did not hear him. The woman and the two men had been sitting in the broad reception room's heavy mission furniture, drinking coffee and talking in low tones. The door opened silently behind them, and the doctor entered. He said, "There will be no further difficulty, comrades. Our patient is in safe hands."

Nelda said, "Won't the orderlies wonder about him?"

Loor shook his head. "I do not feel that I should be required to explain each detail of my activity, dear Nelda, but to bolster your confidence, I will tell you that my staff believes the old man suffers from senile dementia. Should he babble that he is Jaro Capska, Czech delegate to the United Nations, my staff will interpret his ravings as delusions of grandeur and persecution."

Heinz said, "Jaro Capska died yesterday. I read a paper that said he drove his car off a bridge into the East River." He smiled thinly. "No body has been found."

Loor said, "It is too soon. In time a body will be found. At the moment it is in New York being—ah—prepared. When it is found it will have Capska's clothing and rings." He gripped his thighs with his hands. "Not even a wife can identify a man's face after the crabs and eels have worked on it."

Nelda's hand brushed her forehead. She closed her eyes briefly, then opened them and looked at the ceiling. "Our Comrade Minister Capska," she said, as though to herself. "Who would have thought he would try to leave us?"

"Unimportant," Loor said. "What is important is that when his views changed, when he became a collaborator with the bourgeoisie, we were prepared. We knew what to do. We did not fumble and flounder in reaching a decision like your American fools."

The guard who had been silent asked, "Will he confess, Comrade Doctor?"

"Do you doubt it, Comrade Gutierrez? In Prague he will confess. He will *beg* to be permitted the favor of confessing. And he will confess all. To the last name, the last place, the last sum of money, the last comma and period of his filthy chauvinist transactions."

"It is true," Heinz grunted. "I have seen."

Loor said, "But that is not our responsibility. The interrogation will be handled by others to whom it will be a routine affair.

As for ourselves, our responsibility extends further before we are relieved." He looked at the woman. "Comrade Ramos, are you prepared?"

"I am prepared, Comrade Doctor."

"Then you may depart." He looked at his watch. "It is nearly eleven. Do you know the address?"

"As well as I know my own."

"You anticipate no trouble?"

"None whatever. Jake has no more imagination than Heinz."

"Remember, we prefer recruits to forced laborers."

"I'll tell him," she said. "He can make up his own mind."

Heinz and Gutierrez stood up from their chairs. They began walking toward the door. Loor motioned them back. "Replace the furniture, comrades," he said. "Waverly is an institution in which precision is observed." The men carried the chairs to the wall, and waited for Nelda to rise before replacing hers.

Loor said, "Comrade Ramos, we have come a long distance since the fighting in Spain, yet there is a further distance to travel. Together, we shall cover it successfully."

She held out her hand to him. "I am sure of it."

Heinz opened the doors for her, and she went out into the hall. Loor sat in his chair until he heard the heavy car spewing gravel against the porte-cochere, then nose down the spiral road toward the highway. He turned out the hall lights and bolted the front door. Then he stood in the darkness, listening. But from the sound-proofed rooms above there came no sound; not even the dry whistling of an old man's drugged breathing.

Heinz went in first, then Gutierrez. When they had turned off the light over Jake's bed, the woman came in. She locked the door behind her and switched on a flashlight. Then there was the suave *slip-click* of Gutierrez' switch-blade knife opening. The light's cone played over the prostrate figure on the bed. Nelda Ramos said, "Wake him, Heinz."

The guard shuffled toward the bed and gripped the man's shoulders. He pulled them back, then turned the arched body and let it drop against the mattress again. Heinz said, "He's out cold."

"Wake him."

Heinz pulled Jake's body upright and began slapping his face methodically. The opening eyes flickered and shone in the flashlight's beam.

Nelda said, "Jake Webb!" and in his mind there was an awareness of pain and of need; pain from the propeller blade that beat against his face, and need to crawl up and out of the dark pit where he had been lying so that he could answer Nelda's voice. His tongue licked over dry lips, swelling already from Heinz's hand, and he tried to speak. There was a light at the end of the tunnel and he tried to rise so that he could walk toward it, but when he did, something pushed against his chest, and he fell back.

Nelda said, "Enough, Heinz. He's awake now."

"He's still drunk."

"All the better." She shifted the flashlight to her left hand and took out a cigarette. Gutierrez lighted it for her. She said, "Put away your knife. You won't need it."

"He's like a baby," Gutierrez said. "If I cut his throat he'd lie there and drown in his own blood."

She took the knife from his hand and returned the blade to the handle. "Some other time. Save your talent."

Then Webb was aware of an arm around his waist, dragging him to his feet. The light had shifted to the floor, and he realized that he was being half carried to the door. The door opened, and he closed his eyes against the yellow light from the hallway. I'm sick, he told himself. Sick. Must've drunk alky instead of wine. Wine ... The oversweet taste clogged his mouth, bloated his swollen tongue. His toes caught on the stairs and his legs were kicked roughly to free them. The pain reached his thawing mind and he retched. A man's voice cursed him, and then there was another light and the sound of someone coming into the hallway. The voice that spoke was one Webb knew; it was the man who owned the flophouse. It said, "Where you takin' him?"

"Home," Nelda's voice said. "I'm his wife."

"Well, he ain't goin' nowhere till I get that rent that's comin' to me."

"How much is it?"

"Two weeks. Fifteen bucks."

"Here's twenty."

The voice grew respectful. "Well, thanks, lady. You're O.K. Ain't nothin' wrong with your husband. We took good care of him."

She laughed slightly. "They take better care of scrap iron."

He was being dragged again; the light was gone. Cool air fanned his face. Hands lifted his feet, the arms behind him lifted hard, then let him go. He dropped against something soft, yielding. Doors shut metallically. An engine started, its vibration reaching his skull through the window sill against which his head had fallen. The car's sudden forward motion pushed him farther into the cushion; he could feel his hands roll loosely across his knees.

A voice with a Spanish accent said, "Maybe the man give him too much."

Nelda said, "Only a pint. Those were my orders."

"Maybe he was feelin' generous."

"It doesn't take much," she said. "When you don't eat, you can get drunk on a noseful of perfume."

There was the sound of traffic, cars passing in opposite directions; the slick humming of tires against a wet pavement; the powerful pulling of a purring engine. Street lights struck his closed eyelids with rhythmic regularity. The half-heard voices did not interest him. Even though they were talking about him, he felt too detached to care. A huge distance seemed to separate him from the voices; a desert, an ocean, a continent. To mesh his mind in the stream of thought would take more effort, more strength than he could ever collect.

Fingers parted his eyelids, one at a time; light glinted from highly polished nails that looked like pools of wet blood. A hand touched his forehead, his cheek. Nelda's voice said, "Yes, I knew him. He flew with my husband during the war."

"In Spain?"

"No." There was irritation in her voice. "Not Jake. Only Pedro. They were in Africa together, then Italy."

Heinz said, "I was in Africa. Maybe I shot at him."

"Maybe."

Gutierrez said, "This is the one who ran the airline with Pedro."

"Of course," Nelda said.

Heinz asked, "What was the name?"

"Air Caribe. San Juan to Miami and New York."

"Make any dough?"

"At first. But we only had three planes. Jake dunked one of them. Pedro finished off another. That was the end of Air Caribe."

"And Pedro."

"And Pedro."

Gutierrez said, "I was in Ciudad Trujillo then. I remember. It was last year."

Heinz said, "I was in Breslau. Like other Party members, I was busy. When Air Caribe died, I did not notice it."

Gutierrez said, "Air Caribe could have been useful to the Party. Perhaps if—"

Nelda said, "The past is behind. We have work to do now and in the future."

Then the voices were quiet, and of what had been said Jake Webb remembered only words and the inflections of voices—the way foam stays behind when a wave has passed. He had heard clearly, but his mind did not react; no thoughts formed themselves. His will was inert, paralyzed. His brain refused to involve itself in an unequal contest. He wanted only darkness and quiet.

His body sank deeper into the seat as the car lifted into a climbing turn. His ears heard the spatter of gravel against the underbody, and then the car slowed to a stop.

When they left him alone, when the door had clicked shut, when the lights had vanished, when the room was quiet, his mouth could taste the thin bitter liquid they had given him to drink. It covered the inside of his mouth, penetrating each capillary, each pore, each cell, until it had numbed his tongue and his cheeks. His beard grated against the starch-clean pillow. The operating-room smell had made him feel a beginning of shame at the old, accustomed filth of his body, and the softly resilient mattress seemed to cling and grip him, until he knew that he could not move.

Then, in his dream, he felt again the high, quiet peace of a morning above the Tyrrhenian Sea flying from Palermo toward Anzio, seeing the rain clouds ahead, wondering if the chain of gliders behind his plane could stand the buffeting; fighting through the rain, still towing the gliders, until the harbor showed on the radar grid, and when you were searching the grid for the gliders' landing area, the flak began kicking through the clouds, bursting like sickening brown toadstools, while you climbed and the gliders burned or cut loose and plunged into the sea. You had no way of knowing then that the Germans had just bombed the beachhead, and that the Allied guns from ships and the shore were shooting blind at your squadron and its tow of gliders, killing the men who came to help them. And of all the planes, yours was the only one to reach Sicily again, and none of the gliders, of course. Then, after they told you at Palermo what had happened, they court-martialed you for your reply, and took away the silver leaf, exchanging it for a worn gold one you had forgotten to throw away....

He tried to think back, to see the court-martial in perspective, to remember what it had been like, but the door closed, and his mind turned away, searching for the next sequence—something about Pedro and the countless hours in the air over the Caribbean—but it eluded him like quicksilver. Then an endless fog closed around him, smothering his mind until it could remember no more.

When he woke, he did not get up, but lay on his white-enameled hospital bed, looking up at the high wall and the two grilled corner windows. His mind began to function again, to analyze where he was, how he had come here, but the edges were blurred, as though he had swallowed a bottle of aspirin and slept endless hours. The spring sunlight cast grillework shadows on the wall above his bed, but he could not tell from their position whether the time was midmorning or afternoon. He started to look at his wrist watch, but did not draw his wrist from under the covers; the watch had been pawned months ago. It had bought an evening or two of semi-oblivion, and then even that was gone.

What had he done then?

A vague memory of police line-ups until he was identified by someone as a purse-snatcher, by another as the thief who had stolen and sold two tires. Stronger memories came into his mind: a gray cell and food whose smell made you vomit; a stench of skin and sweat and louse-ridden dungarees; a turnkey in blue uniform and visored hat who woke you at night by kicking you; who whispered filthy things you had not believed existed; then, finally, a day when the door opened and you walked out on the street again and found your friends sharing a gallon of Napa Valley white, spiked with smoke.

His stomach started to contract, and his body began to ache for a drink. It seemed as though his veins were expanding, readying themselves for the intake of alcohol his system craved. His pulse pounded, sweat formed on his forehead; his muscles tensed themselves; a pool of saliva formed under his tongue. This was different from wanting a woman; different, and yet alike in the demanding need for satisfaction. It was worse, because a cold shower could not help. You could forget desire in an hour, but the need for wine grew and swelled, pyramided and exploded in a frenzy that would not be denied.

His hands clenched into fists; dirty nails dug into his palms. His body stiffened and he looked at the ceiling in terror.

What if he could not get a drink?

Something hung from the bedpost by his right shoulder. It looked like a shrunken white pear with a mother-of-pearl button in the end. He clawed at it, pressing the button with his thumb. Somewhere, distantly, a chime sounded.

His hand released its grip, and he waited in agony until he could hear the rhythmic brushing of rubber heels on linoleum. Then his door was opened.

A man came in.

The man wore an intern's half-sleeve white jacket. He was about thirty-five, and his cleanly shaven face glinted metallically as his jaw moved. He said, "How do you feel, Mr. Webb?"

"I want a drink."

The man came toward him and took his pulse.

Webb said, "Listen, I've got to have a drink."

The man nodded. He was watching his wrist watch, counting. When he finished, he said, "What kind of a drink?"

"Anything. Wine, gin, whisky, bay rum—anything that's got the stuff in it.

"Before breakfast?"

"I'm not like other people. I don't need to eat. Just let me have a drink."

The man sat on the bed and examined Webb's eyes. "Let's get things straight," he said. "This isn't a cocktail lounge. This is the Waverly Rest Home. You're here for treatment."

"What kind of treatment?"

"Alcoholism," the man said.

Terror clawed at his intestines. "You mean I can't have a drink?"

"I didn't say that. I said you're here for treatment. You'll have alcohol for a while—then no more. By the time you're ready to leave, you'll hate the sight of a beer bottle. The smell of gin will sicken you."

"I'm sick now. I need a drink, I tell you. Now!" He had risen on his elbows, his hands plucking at the covers.

The man pushed him back against the pillow, very gently. "You'll get your drink now, Mr. Webb, but before you get the next one, you'll have to eat."

"Get me a drink!"

The man went out of the room, closing the door behind him. Webb tried to shut his eyes, to forget the craving that consumed him, but his mind was focused on the sound of footsteps coming toward the room, the door opening again.

A nurse came in. She was young and not very pretty. Pleasantly she said, "Dr. Selby says you're to drink this, Mr. Webb." She gave him a small beaker. It was filled with something almost colorless. His nose caught the life-giving scent as he sat up and reached for it. The beaker grated against his teeth as he tilted it hurriedly and drank until nothing remained.

The nurse took the glass from him as he coughed and bent forward. The liquor seemed to etch its path into his stomach; its fumes filled his lungs chokingly, and he gasped for air.

She said, "You'll feel better now, Mr. Webb."

He lay back against the pillow, breathing heavily. "I'm sure of it. That was real applejack."

"One hundred proof," she said.

He could feel the liquor take hold, filling the empty veins, the slack muscles of his body; hardening his cortex until his body seemed to vibrate with health.

Dr. Selby had come from somewhere and was standing beside the bed, holding a hypodermic syringe. The nurse bared Webb's left arm, and the injection was completed quickly, efficiently.

"What's that for?" Webb asked.

"It's a sedative. Your body has got to become accustomed to not being stimulated by alcohol."

"I wouldn't like that."

"You don't have to."

Webb felt hostile to Dr. Selby and the prim, unattractive nurse. "I don't have to stay here," he said. "I can go any time I want to go."

"You'll like it here. The drinks are free."

Webb's mind seemed to have become suddenly clear, integrated with the muscular potential of his revivified body. "Who brought me here?" he asked. "What happened to me?"

Selby shrugged. "I thought you might remember. Mrs. Ramos arranged for your admission."

Webb said nothing for a moment. Then, "Why?"

"I didn't ask her. She's a friend of Dr. Loor."

"Who's he?"

The nurse tittered. "Dear me," she said. "Oh, dear me." She looked helplessly at Dr. Selby.

Selby said, "Dr. Loor owns Waverly." He opened the door and the nurse brushed past him, into the corridor.

Webb said, "Where's Mrs. Ramos? Where's Nelda?"

"She didn't confide in me," Selby said. "Anyway, who'd want to look at you the way you are now?" He walked into the corridor, and the door closed behind him.

The glow of Webb's body began to be overshadowed by a feeling of compelling relaxation. The blood that had been racing through his veins slowed to an unaccustomed, pleasurable languor. A wave of calm came over him, and when an orderly came in to wash and shave him, Webb did not protest.

His body clean, his face free of the matted grime that had served to mask him from the world, Webb closed his eyes and tried to sleep. Almost forgotten patterns of thought re-established themselves in his brain. The dead past rose from its grave and beckoned toward him, and as he drew nearer, he saw that the figure in the coffin was Nelda. Her death mask was only a false face worn for *El Día de Los Muertos*—the Day of the Dead. As she rose to come toward him, he could see the name on a tombstone beside the grave in which she had been lying: "Pedro Ramos, 1910-1948," and the flowers he had brought fell across the grave, and then Nelda was standing in front of him, saying, "He's dead now, Jake."

"I know."

"His plane crashed off Cape Cabron."

"I'll never see Pedro again."

"No one will, Jake darling. There's nothing to keep us apart."

"Nothing."

"Then why don't we go away together? I've known all these months that you wanted me."

"Have you?"

"Yes. Yes."

"Not now, Nelda. It's too soon. Maybe later."

"Now."

"No."

He saw the glint of a knife in her hand, the death mask fusing suddenly with her features, the thin black gauze falling from her breasts, the revelation of the white unmarked body, the hollow of her thorax, the tapering mound of her belly, and he felt revulsion in his throat at the thought of taking a woman returned from the graveyard, like an undertaker's assistant. But the knife turned to smoke, the death mask dissolved, the lewd body sank into its coffin, and in his mind was only the memory of desire unrealized. Nelda, who swam with him and Pedro at night, brushing against him in the warm water, catching her thigh against his, touching her breast to his arm, kissing him clingingly underwater, holding him with her hands when Pedro could not see. All of this done in calculated, coldblooded lust without the saving grace of headstrong passion; done to confuse, to embarrass, to inflame, to take—without giving.

The dream overcame him, and his mind drifted away, blanketed in a montage of memories and fantasy. In time the dream resolved itself and he slept peacefully, without drug-evoked images, secure from the loneliness of silent sorrow, seeing only a vast depth of black that absorbed even the flickerings of thought.

He could see her dimly, silhouetted against the wall as she sat beside him on the bed. The dream had merged with reality, and in the half-darkness of the room he could make out the shape of her head, black hair parted in the middle and swept to each side with rolled braids over the ears. As she turned, he could see the profile of her body, accentedly feminine. The sound of his head brushing the pillow made her look down. She said, "Jake."

"Yes."

"How do you feel?"

"I'm all right. I've been sleeping."

"I know."

"Why am I here?"

"Maybe I just wanted to see you again."

"No. There's more than that."

She leaned toward him, and her perfume was like bougainvillea at night. "Let's say I wanted to see you for old times' sake."

"I don't believe it. Why have you been sitting here?"

He could see the half shrug of her shoulders. "They said you were calling my name in your sleep."

"Was I? I don't remember."

She leaned closer to him, and he could feel her shoulders against his, her cheek beside his ear. Her lips said, "I've found a road back for you, Jake. Maybe it's wide enough for both of us."

He shook his head. “I don’t understand, Nelda. I was through—finished. A few more weeks and it’d have been over with. Why pull me back?”

In the silence before she spoke, he could hear her accelerated breathing. He became aware of her body against his. She whispered, “Perhaps I wanted to see what finally became of the man who thought himself too good to take me when I offered myself.”

“Is that all?”

She shook her head. “Only part of it.” Her hand touched his forehead. “I wanted you once, Jake. Maybe I’ll want you again. But not until you’re cured. Not until they lower you into hell and make you climb back by yourself.”

CHAPTER TWO

After sleep came awakening. He was surprised again to find himself in the clean, white-walled room. His clearing mind formed the words Waverly Rest Home, and the slight knowledge that he knew where he was became strangely satisfying.

When he rang for the nurse, she came in. He said, "I'd like a bathrobe and slippers. I want to get up."

She went to a closet and brought back a lightweight blue wool bathrobe and a pair of terry-cloth slippers. "Anything else, Mr. Webb?"

"Sure. A drink."

The nurse smiled smugly. "Not until you've eaten."

"I'm not hungry."

She turned on her heel. "No eat, no drink."

"To hell with you."

"All right, if that's how you want it."

"No… Hell, it's not your fault." He threw off the covers and put the bathrobe around his shoulders. "Where's Dr. Selby?"

"He isn't on duty yet."

Webb put his feet into the slippers. "I need a drink." He looked at his hands. They were white, unhealthily so. The taut veins stood out like pipe lines.

The nurse said, "You're going to have to get used to doing without liquor, Mr. Webb. You might as well start now."

He looked at her. "You like that, don't you? You like the thought of having something somebody wants." His eyes traveled over the thin, angular body. "Well, enjoy yourself. I'll bet it's the first time you had something a man wanted."

The nurse caught her breath and her face reddened. She went quickly out of the room. Webb walked slowly to the door, feeling weak and suddenly tired. He tried the handle, but the spring lock was controlled from the other side. He sat on the bed for a moment, resting and looking at the locked door, the grilled windows. "Like a zoo," he said. "Just like a goddamned zoo." He began to laugh, lightly at first, then louder, until his lungs hurt, until his throat began to contract and he coughed uncontrollably.

Looking for water, he stumbled toward the closet door, opened it, and saw a small bathroom. He ran water into a plastic cup and drank it in short gulps. Finally he stopped coughing. The exertion had dizzied him and he leaned against the washbowl while his head cleared. A stainless-steel shower stall stood in one corner beside a toilet. He turned toward the medicine cabinet over the basin and saw his face in the mirror. At least, it looked enough like a face he remembered to be his. It was white and thin, with flesh clinging to cheekbones, brown eyes almost cavernous. The sight startled him. He bared his teeth; they were stained, the gums pale and shrunken. He thought, I look like my father, not myself. I look the way my old man did the day they buried him. And my hair hangs like Spanish moss. He ran his hand through his hair, pushing it back from his forehead. I need a drink and a haircut, and then another drink. He looked at his face again, and turned away. I know what I really need, he told himself. I need three squares a day for a couple of weeks, some sun, and a lot of sleep. That's what I really need. More than a haircut; even more than a drink.

He heard a noise in the room and saw Dr. Selby come in. Two men followed him. One was solid and beefy, his pink face square and expressionless. The other was shorter and thin; his skin was olive, his hair oily and long. Ringlets curled down the side of his neck.

Selby was coolly professional. He stood, blocking the door, and said, "I hear you don't want to co-operate."

"I won't argue."

"Don't be snotty with the nurse, Webb. She's only doing her job."

"Yeah? Just what is her job?"

"She's not a bartender." He half turned, so that Webb could see the other two. "If you don't like Miss Porter, I can arrange to have Heinz and Gutierrez look after you."

"I'll take Miss Porter."

"You're smart."

"Not particularly. Your friends look pretty ugly. They're even uglier than the nurse."

Heinz scowled. Selby laughed shortly. "They're plenty ugly. Heinz used to interrogate prisoners for Rommel, and Gutierrez graduated from the Caribbean Legion."

"He's lucky," Webb said. "The way I heard it, there wasn't enough left of the Caribbean Legion to shoot at."

Gutierrez tried to push past Selby. In Spanish he said, "I'll cut his heart out."

In English, Webb said, "We'll have our day, pachuco. Sometime when your ugly friend isn't around to back you up."

Selby pushed Gutierrez away from the door. To Webb he said, "You sound like you might have had guts. Once upon a time."

"Do I?" Webb dropped the bathrobe and pulled the hospital shirt over his head. "I used to weigh a hundred and eighty. How much do you figure me now?"

Selby looked at him, and Webb could not help looking at his own ribs, his breastbone, the sharp concave of his thorax. Selby said, "Forty, maybe. No more."

"I could use some weight," Webb said. "I'll start with a drink."

"I'm the doctor," Selby said. "You'll get your drink, but first you'll eat breakfast."

Webb shrugged. "You're the doctor."

Selby turned and motioned the men out of the room. "Stay sensible," he said. "I can make this easy for you."

"Why?"

"Why what?"

"Why should you make it easy for me? Why should Nelda bring me here? Why should I be here at all?"

Selby turned and walked toward the door. "You'll hear about it," he said. "Someone's got plans for you."

"Like what?"

"Like putting you on the wagon for good; like bringing back your health and your nerve."

Webb leaned back against the washbowl again. "Why?"

Selby laughed thinly. "Why? So you can fly a plane. That's why."

After breakfast he tried nursing the drink. He had forced down a boiled egg, part of a piece of ham, and a slice of toast. He could not remember a meal when he had eaten more. The liquor burned his tongue, corroded his throat. He savored it like brandy, holding off the moment when it would be finished, pretending that there was more in a bottle in the bureau, that a friend would stop by with a pint and some lemons, or that he had money enough to buy a can of Sterno and a loaf of bread. (You hold the Sterno over a candle until it melts, then pour it through the bread to strain out the poison that blinds and kills.) But he knew that he had no money, no friends with a pint, and when he finished the last quarter inch he would have drunk his ration for the entire day.

When the thought goaded him unbearably, he tilted the beaker and swallowed. Then he put the beaker on the night table and lay back on the bed. Almost at once the old well-remembered glow came over him. He was rich, he was successful, he was happy. He owned an airline that covered the hemisphere from Santiago to Bermuda. The planes were fast new Martins, not limping, war-weary C-46's. They could kick off three hundred and climb above a storm. They had pressurized cabins and stewards and navigational aids and good ground crews and ticket offices and international advertising—everything Air Caribe had lacked.

He remembered Pedro talking about Air Caribe for the first time. They had been drinking coffee in a ready room at the Blida airdrome in Algiers, and Pedro told him how many Puerto Rican workers wanted to come to the United States. A nonscheduled airline could cut prices, fly the Puerteños to Miami and New York for maybe a hundred bucks a head, and still make money. In New York the Puerteños could go on relief until they got jobs and learned how to speak English. After all, they were citizens, and Marcantonio would take care of them. They'd make more money than in Puerto Rico and Air Caribe would be performing a public service.

How good it sounded! Webb thought. How fine it was to sit in North Africa planning your own airline, hearing how Pedro's uncles would lend him enough dough to put a down payment on some surplus planes after the war. He had saved twelve thousand from the war, and that added to Pedro's dough and the money his uncles lent Air Caribe bought three C-46's. He had gassed them and flown them one at a time with Pedro from Arizona to Miami and San Juan, and Pedro had handled the CAB licensing, and suddenly one morning there was Air Caribe, and the sugarcane workers were lined up outside the hangar waiting to climb aboard the waiting plane.

The door opened and Miss Porter came in, carrying some pills on a small tray. When she had put them on the night table, she poured a glass of water, and started to leave. Webb said, "I'm sorry, Nurse. I'm co-operating."

She turned and looked at him. "That's nice, Mr. Webb. Everything will be much easier. The pills are vitamins."

"That was a good drink. I feel better."

She looked at him curiously. "You look better," she said. "I've never had a drink. My family didn't believe in drinking. It's hard for me to understand what liquor can mean to people."

Webb took the pills in the palm of his hand, swallowed them, and washed them down with water. "It's like sleeping pills," he said. "Something happens and you need them. Then you can't do without. That's the way it is with me."

She came back to the bed and straightened the pillows. "You're young," she said. "You'll get over it."

"I haven't tried."

"You won't have to for a while. Not until you're stronger, anyway. You need food now more than anything. Why, you're half starved."

"I can't remember being hungry."

"That's the trouble with liquor; it starves you without your knowing it. I won't say you'll have an easy time, Mr. Webb, but Dr. Selby's done this lots of times."

"I suppose you've had a lot of alcoholics here."

Miss Porter nodded. "Dope addicts, too."

"Dope costs too much. I thought about it, but I didn't have the money."

She paused at the door and looked at him again. "You're really a nice man," she said. "You probably even went to college."

"University of Washington."

"For heaven's sake! I come from Portland."

"Practically neighbors," Webb said. He was finding being pleasant almost quite of an effort.

"I left Portland during the war." She tilted her head slightly. "I suppose you were in the war."

"Yes."

"Where?"

"Africa. Italy. I was a flyer."

"Oh."

Webb lay back again. "I'm tired," he said. "If I sleep do I get another drink?"

"Not today. But you'll sleep anyway. You're on sedatives for the rest of the week."

"That'll help," Webb said. "When I wake up I'll ring."

"Do that," she said, and closed the door.

After a while Webb remembered looking for a razor just before breakfast, then ringing for the orderly, who brought him an electric shaver. He had never liked them, but now that his face was clean he wanted to keep it that way. He had begun to prize cleanliness and sleep. Webb knew that they were keeping razor blades from him. Hell, who'd trust a wino?

The feeling of well-being had reached his feet and his hands. The liquor and the sedative combined to slow his breathing. Before he fell asleep he saw a bird perch on the window grille, resting a moment in its flight.

In Webb's dream he was floating on the Caribbean in a yellow rubber life raft. He was alone, without food or water. In his signaling mirror he could see his rail-thin body, the fleshless ribs curving laterally like branches of a fire-scorched pine. Thirst grew; night came and went, and in the blazing morning two birds flew toward him. He tried to cry out, thinking that because of the birds he was near land, but the birds flew closer, blotting the sun with their wings, and he saw that they were birds of prey; huge vultures, grotesque and without pity. He was too weak to kill them for the liquid of their blood, and each hour that they circled overhead he lay a little lower in the raft, shrinking from the moment when they would glide low and perch beside his body.

As he watched their relentless orbiting they came nearer, and he could see their heads and their faces: the gaunt, dark pachuco, and the red-faced Kraut. Before the knives in their talons slashed into his body, he begged them for a drink....

He woke, sweating, turned on the light, and sat up in bed. His throat was dry as garnet paper; his cheeks felt sunken, sucked inward from thirst. His hand trembled as he reached for the thermos jug on the night table. He drank a glass, then a second, but the cool water did not satisfy him. As he lay back and stared at the ceiling he knew that nothing would satisfy him but a long pull from a bottle. He resented his surroundings, hated the cleanliness that stared at him from white walls. The sterility of the room seemed to scream at him that within these walls he was to suffer and that tonight was the beginning of his torture—payment for what he knew not.

His body was sweating now. The sheets clung to the backs of his thighs as he searched for coolness. The trembling advanced through his arms, his torso, his neck and legs, and when he could stand it no longer, he rang for the orderly.

The orderly's face looked like curdled milk. It seemed to swirl as though a bug were swimming in it, then the broken nose took shape halfway between two torn, crumpled ears. He looked like a sparring partner who lost every fight. His voice said, "Whaddaya want?"

"I want a drink."

The pug laughed. "Ain't that a shame? It's after midnight and the bartender's gone home."

"Give me a drink, you ugly bastard. Dr. Selby lets me have it."

"Yeah? Well, I ain't looked at your chart yet, sweetheart, but they don't generally bring characters here to keep 'em sauced up."

"I'm different. I'm a special patient." His nails ground into his palms. His spine arched like a trout rod.

The laugh echoed hollowly in the white prison room. "You're all special patients, sweetheart. You're all special or you wouldn't be here." He looked at Webb and his milk-water eyes crawled like beetles. "Maybe you're tellin' the trut', though. I'll take a chance because you're so pretty. Just lie back on your pillow and think pretty thoughts until I get back." He walked to the door and went out into the hall.

Webb, waiting for the door's familiar click, did not hear it this time. Turning his head, he saw the hall light through the crevice of the open door. Fear that Milk Face would not bring the drink gripped him. It quieted his body, steadied his nerve, cleared his mind, and without realizing what he was doing, he stepped unsteadily onto the cold floor and eased out into the hall.

Twenty feet away sat the nurses' desk, the night light shaded by a stack of papers. The orderly was somewhere beyond the range of Webb's hearing. A window at the end of the corridor was open, but barred from the outside. Spring air blew against Webb's body, chilling him, and he moved quickly. A small refrigerator stood beside the night desk and he opened it quietly, but there was nothing inside that looked even remotely like liquor. He cursed softly and closed the refrigerator door. Looking over his shoulder, he saw what looked like an instrument case farther down the hall, half hidden by shadows. He knew that time was running out on him, and he crouched into a run that brought him up beside the glass-and-steel case, breathing heavily. The cold sweat on his palms made his hands slip as he tried to turn the slick steel knobs, and when he realized that the cabinet was locked, his heart began to pound in desperation. He put his entire weight on one of the knobs and saw it bend. The rolled-steel door-fame began to warp outward and the glass pane starred and cracked. A piece fell to the floor, breaking again and spattering his feet with cold fragments. His eyes were becoming accustomed to the light, and he could see bottles and flasks inside the cabinet. His fingers tore at the broken pane, trying to widen the hole so that his hand could reach inside and bring back a bottle, but fear doubled his fist and pushed it through the pane with a crash.

The hand reached for a bottle, a brown one, and drew it back outside the shattered case. Blood dripped onto the bottle's neck as he fumbled with the cork, and then as it tilted upward, something wrenched it from his hand and buckled his knees from behind. From the floor he looked dazedly upward at the orderly. The orderly replaced the bottle inside the cabinet and said, "I didn't figure you quite right, sweetheart. You don't look like you got strength enough to pull up the covers."

Hands in his armpits jerked him to his feet and propelled him back toward the white-walled room. The harsh voice said, "You don't get no sauce, sweetheart. You had yours."

Webb turned his head. "That was this morning." His teeth had begun to chatter.

"Don't gimme no more trouble. You had your drink. That's it. Period."

"I can't do without it."

The pug laughed. "You guys kill me. All of you. Soft bastards who can't do without women or sauce. So you wind up here, where you can't get neither one." He pushed open the door of Webb's room and closed it behind him. "Get into bed," he said.

Webb got into bed.

"I'll be back, sweetheart, an' I wouldn't move if I was you—not a curly chest hair." He went out of the room, and the door swung shut. The lock clicked with finality.

Webb tried to bury himself under the light covers. His body was shaking uncontrollably now; his skin felt as though it were covered with frozen eels. His stomach had twisted itself inside out, and his throat was no larger than a straw. He brought his knees up to his chest, crossed his forearms across his chest, and began to sob nervously.

The door swung open again, and Milk Face came in. "Feelin' bad, sweetheart?" the voice taunted. "Just pass me part of an arm, and you'll grow ten foot tall."

Webb turned so that he could see the hypodermic in the blunt hand. The knuckles looked like old golf balls. He said, "What's that?"

"Sauce," Milk Face said. "We'll just feed a vein and short-cut your throat." He gripped Webb's nearest arm and jabbed in the needle.

Almost at once, warmth flooded outward from the pin point of pain. It coursed down the veins to his clenched hand, relaxed it and doubled back through Webb's chest, his neck, head, and body. He closed his eyes and felt rough fingers fumbling with his right hand. Something was being twisted around it. Suddenly he remembered cutting himself painfully on the glass cabinet.

Then there was no pain any more, no sensation but smooth brushing friction as Milk Face bandaged his hand. The voice said, "You ain't got too much blood, sweetheart. Leave the bandage on. The way you look now, you couldn't stand a nosebleed."

"—yourself," Webb said.

The pug laughed. "I don't need to, sweetheart. That's your problem." He turned off the light and went out of the door into the hall. The door clicked shut so quietly that Webb's dulling ears hardly heard it.

Then he was alone in the dark, quiet room, but he did not care. Fear was gone. Pain had vanished, and there was only a feeling of immense well-being. His searching mind seemed to soar beyond the quietness of the room, away from the darkness and the loneliness, until he was high above the clouds in the warmth of a C-46 cabin, feeling the throttle knobs under his hand, the soft pressure of rudder pedals against the soles of his fur-lined flying boots. The sun strained through his dark goggles, and he tried to look away from it, but against his will his head was turned toward the source of light. He pulled back on the controls and the plane began to climb. He adjusted the propellers' pitch so that they would bite deeper into the thin, cold air. Then he sat back in the cushioned seat and waited while his plane climbed toward the sun.

Morning came late, and with it a succession of white uniforms bringing fluoroscopes, metal standards, glass slides, plastic trays, X-ray machines, syringes that took from his blood, other syringes that added to it, bottles of plasma and sucrose that inverted and fed into his veins, hands that counted his pulse, measured the pressure of his blood, and finally left behind them a vacuum into which his weary mind crawled for refuge.

The next day the multitude did not probe him, peer at him, or thrust thermometers under his tongue. The bandage on his hand was taken off, the cuts dusted with sulfa powder and forgotten. His breath had become rank, and a nurse told him it was because of the huge vitamin doses his body was absorbing. Breakfast and lunch went down easier. He remembered to ask for his drink after lunch, and when it came, he knew after the first taste that it had been cut with water. Drinking it slowly, savoring its last moisture, he knew that there would be less and less from now on as his health returned.

His sleep became almost dreamless, the craving for alcohol slackening as the intravenous feeding filled the void that alcohol once had filled. By the time he found himself wanting food, he had lost track of time. The days had faded into a montage of faces, medicines, and dreamless sleep. Liquor came to him regularly, but now it was nothing more than the smell of a cork passed over the beaker. Then one afternoon Dr. Selby came in carrying a hypodermic.

Webb put down his book and said, "Give or take?"

"Give," Selby said. "If you can take this you'll be on your feet and ready to go."

"What is it?"

"Antabuse."

Webb shook his head. "Never heard of it."

Selby swabbed an arm with alcohol—denatured. "It's something new. From Sweden." He sank the needle into Webb's tricep. It seemed to hit the bone.

"What's it for?"

"Alcoholism," Selby said. He massaged the muscle. "Flex you arm."

"How does it work?"

"We aren't sure. It's a new substance. Basically, it conditions your system to reject anything that contains alcohol."

"Like what?"

"Like making you throw up the next time you take a drink."

Webb laughed. "Try me."

Selby dropped the syringe into a chest pocket. "We will, friend. We'll try very soon."

"It sounds crazy. I don't believe it'll work."

"It may not, with you, but I think it will. That is, if you're one of the eight out of ten it works on."

"I'm normal."

Selby gestured toward the bathroom. "Take a shower and they'll bring you some clean clothes."

"For what?"

"You can't lie here the rest of your life. Part of the cure depends on your body's becoming normal again. You've got to walk, to exercise—slowly at first, then like a stevedore."

"Good."

"What do you like to do?"

"Fish. Hunt."

"I mean sports."

"I boxed a little."

Selby shook his head. "No good. Ever wrestle?"

"In flying school. Why?"

"It builds muscles. Boxing doesn't. Take a walk today, but go easy. Tomorrow, do more if you feel like it."

When Webb came out of the shower, the clothes were on his bed: a heavy white cotton sweat suit with the name Waverly stenciled on the back and legs in black ink. New sneakers and sweat socks completed the wardrobe. He dressed and rang the buzzer. Milk Face came in.

Webb said, "Where do we go?"

"Not far, sweetheart. There's what they call an orchard out back. You're supposed to walk there until you've counted every tree."

"What then?"

"Then you come back and tell me how many trees you counted."

"That's a waste of time," Webb said. "How would you know if the number was right or wrong?" He walked toward the open door and out into the corridor. He made it to the nurses' desk before he began feeling dizzy, then he angled toward the wall and leaned toward it, brushing it with his hand as he walked. Milk Face, behind him, said, "You won't go far today, sweetheart. You can't even make it outside the building, can you?"

"I can make it." His breath was coming hard now, and his blood was pounding in his lungs, inside his head. His feet seemed to have picked up a load of wet cement. He dragged them sluggishly over the smooth linoleum and down winding steps to a barred metal door that opened onto a tree-covered field. Before he opened the door, he breathed deeply, gulping air to slow the beating of his heart.

His first step on the soft ground was uncertain. Webb felt the sneakers sink into the rain-moist turf, heard their sucking sound as he walked forward. Beyond him the cherry trees were outlined against the sky. As he walked toward them, the breeze played at his throat like tendrils of ivy. The fresh smell of outside air seemed almost unreal; he was so accustomed to the sick-ward scent of his room that his nostrils contracted and his lungs seemed to shrivel.

The trees grew in seven long rows that curved down the side of the hill. He knew that he would not walk to the far end of the rows this time, because climbing back up the hill would take too much out of him. As he walked he did not try to count the trees. Instead, he noticed the grotesque silhouettes of the trees, their branches rigid in supplication toward the sky, like burned, contorted corpses. He had seen a Focke Wulf crash in the desert at Sidi-el-Beb, and when he had reached it with the crash crew half an hour later, the longerons and stringers were so intermingled with the blackened skeletons that they used a bulldozer to push a burial mound over the wreckage.

It was horrors like that one that made him loathe the war, made him pray for a day of peace when he could strip off his uniform and start flying civilians with Pedro over the Caribbean.

He rubbed his hands together to warm them and licked his drug-chapped lips. A field mouse streaked for cover as he trod near its nest, and in the distance he could hear birds singing. It seemed years to him since he had been out of doors. He could hardly remember spending a day in the woods. Instead, his memories were of days and nights along the Embarcadero, sponging drinks; sleeping in the half shelter of doorways; buying nickel hamburgers drenched with free ketchup; wanting only to bridge the fog-filled chasm between today and tomorrow. Now that he had been brought part way back to normal existence, a long dead curiosity began to bait him. He was not thinking any longer of the future as something to be kept from his thoughts. He could not help wondering what Nelda had planned for him; what Selby had meant when he said that Webb was being reconditioned so that he could fly once more.

Webb shook his head. He had no idea where his pilot's license was, or his instrument rating card. And even if he had them, there would be weeks of refamiliarization needed before the CAA would let him handle commercial controls again. He wondered if he could even pass the physical tests. Something could have happened to his heart or his lungs or his blood pressure while he was destroying himself with wine and smoke. And his nerves would have to get a hell of a lot steadier than they were. Now that he thought about the obstacles, they seemed insurmountable; not worth the struggle.

Webb stopped under a cherry tree and held onto a low branch to rest. From the bay came the sound of a ship's whistle, high and tremulous and distant. The slope of the land gave him an idea of where he was, but he found himself with no desire to try to run away. Even if he wanted to, he knew that Milk Face could overtake him in a matter of minutes; that someone was probably watching him from the big stone building.

As he stood immobile beside the trunk of the tree, he saw three figures pass the end of the orchard a hundred feet away, walking toward the sanitarium. Webb did not move. He watched them go slowly across the field, his eyes scrutinizing Heinz and Gutierrez, his mind wondering who the man was between them. Webb could see enough of the man's muffled head to see an expanse of short white beard, a thin sensitive nose, a high curving forehead whose intelligence potential contrasted markedly with those of the two escorts. Webb did not need a better look to know that the man was old. Age bent his shoulders, slowed his steps, and made them uncertain as he picked his way over the soft ground. Once he half stumbled, but Heinz's quick arm straightened his body and he plodded the rest of the way to the door without incident. Webb did not move until the door had closed behind them. Then he turned and made his way slowly back to the building.

He slept until dinnertime, and when he woke he found that he had an appetite. But even after eating his meal, he was not satisfied. A nerve-deep craving made his legs twitch, his mouth turn dry.

Miss Porter answered his ring, and when she saw his empty tray she smiled happily. "I guess we're feeling better, Mr. Webb."

"We're feeling lousy."

"Oh? Is something wrong?"

His yearning was too intense for joking. He said, "I need a drink."

He thought that something like pity crossed her face.

She said, "Please try not to drink any more."

"I can't. I've got to have it."

"You won't like it, Mr. Webb."

"The hell I won't. Just give it to me."

"You've forgotten the antabuse."

"No, I haven't. It won't work on me."

Miss Porter opened the door. "I'll come right back," she said. "I'll bring a bottle."

"Make it fast." He lay on the bed feeling his palms begin to grow slick, his mouth salivating in anticipation. He played a game of counting, betting with himself that she would open the door on the count of twenty—thirty—forty-five—sixty—seventy-eight and the door opened. Miss Porter brought a bottle and a glass to the bed. Webb hardly looked at the label, and when he drank, he did not use the glass.

The liquor had hardly settled in his stomach before his body began to react. A cold chill shook him, and his stomach turned over warningly. Webb handed the bottle back to Miss Porter and got out of bed. He barely made it to the toilet before he threw up. His body shook in a spasm of vomiting, and Webb dropped to his knees as he began to shake uncontrollably. His head was the size of the room; his stomach was a balloon that had detached itself from his intestines and was spinning like a cement mixer, slopping its contents over his lips. Spots revolved before his eyes as he retched until his stomach had emptied itself and there was only the bitter taste of bile.

His body was too weak to support itself. In a paroxysm of shivering, Webb lay back on the tile floor and tried to draw the bath mat over himself for warmth.

From the door a voice said, "Feelin' bad, sweetheart?"

Webb opened his eyes and saw the room sway.

"You'll catch cold on the floor, sweetheart. Here, I'll tuck you back in bed."

"—yourself," Webb said. He heard Milk Face's heels scrape over the floor, felt strong arms lift him and carry him into the room.

The orderly pulled the covers over Webb and turned off the light. "I think you'll sleep good," he said, "but if you a need a drink, pour yourself one any time. The bottle's handy on the table."

The door closed and Webb turned on the bed light. The bottle was there on the table, two feet away. As he looked at it, he could feel himself getting sick again. He switched off the light and closed his eyes.

CHAPTER THREE

IN THE NEXT two weeks they gave Webb massages, sunlamp treatments, and supervised exercise. Sleep came without drugs, then the rediscovery of his body as a well-knit entity capable of lifting weights, pulling oars, matching muscles with Milk Face.

His face was tanned and free of the hunger lines that had webbed it before he was brought to Waverly. The new clothes that Nelda brought him fitted closely around his taut midriff and lay smoothly across his squared shoulders. Ten pounds more and Webb would be at his Air Force weight.

One afternoon Miss Porter told him that Mrs. Ramos would meet him in the reception room, and when Webb had changed to outdoor clothing he walked quickly to meet her. She sat on a leather-covered sofa, smoking a cigarette, arranging a yellow foulard scarf around her coiled black hair. She looked up at Webb and said, "Quite a change, Jake."

"I was due for one."

She rose and came toward him. "How do you feel?"

"Sober."

"Anything else?"

"Broke."

"I can change that."

"How?"

She offered him a cigarette and he shook his head. "We're taking a little drive, Jake. It's time we had a talk."

"Alone?"

She laughed. "Almost. Heinz and Silvio will ride the rear seat. If company means brains, we'll be alone."

"Who's Silvio, the pachuco?"

She nodded. "He doesn't like being called that."

"Then shave off his sideburns and take away his knife."

Nelda took his arm and they walked toward the door. "That's a man's job, Jake. I'll leave it for you."

The maroon Lincoln convertible rounded the high curve and pulled off the road into a clearing in the trees. Below them in the distance they could see the Presidio, and beyond, the bay. A cool spring wind blew through the open convertible. Nelda pushed back her scarf, patted the braids coiled over her ears, and opened the door. Webb looked back at the two-man escort. "Why don't you boys just sit here and swap dirty stories?" He got out of the car and met Nelda beside the door. Heinz sat forward and lighted a cigar. He said to Nelda, "Think you can handle him, comrade?"

"I'm the only one who can."

"You know what Dr. Loor said."

"I know *everything* Dr. Loor said. However, I have a certain advantage in knowing Mr. Webb better than anyone else. If I thought he might be tempted to abuse our hospitality, I would take proper precautions."

Webb smiled. "Like what? Leg irons and hound dogs?"

"Hardly. Modem methods are more efficient, if less picturesque."

Heinz said, "Just the same, comrade, we'll be here if you need us."

"Quite right. That's why you were told to come." Nelda took Webb's arm and they began walking toward the trees.

When they were out of sight of the Lincoln, Nelda spread her scarf over a blanket of pine needles. She sat down and Webb crossed his legs Indian fashion. When she had lighted a cigarette she said, "You look wonderful, Jake. I didn't know Waverly could work miracles."

"Apparently it can."

"Yes," she said. "I think you've got it licked. The liquor, I mean."

"Take antabuse for a while. See how much sauce you want."

"No, thanks. I still like a friendly Gibson."

"Sounds like a dirty word."

Nelda lay back, pillowing her head on her hands. "There's a lot of past behind us, Jake. Pedro, Air Caribe, Puerto Rico, Skid Row. The question is, what's to become of the future?"

He shrugged. "You were going to tell me."

"I will. The world has changed, Jake. There's more to living than running a two-bit airline, sweating out your load-mile loss."

"For instance."

"For instance, getting on the winning side. Picking the winners early enough so that when the smoke blows away you'll have everything you've ever dreamed of. Using your knowledge, your skill and talent for something bigger than another Air Caribe."

"Keep talking."

"It's getting in on the ground floor of an irresistible power that's destined to sweep the world."

"Television?"

She shook her head angrily. "Be serious, Jake. It's the people's will."

"I see."

"You're smart, Jake. You always were. I don't have to go on. You know what I'm talking about."

He nodded.

"I've recruited others, Jake. By the dozens. I know the sales talk, the Party line. If I were ordered to, I could convince the Rockefellers."

"It's that good?"

She nodded. "And you—you don't really have any alternative."

"I could say no. I could get up and walk away and you'd never see me again."

She shook her head slowly. "No, Jake. Even if you could get past Heinz and Silvio—which I doubt—the Party would find you. We found you once."

"That was easy. I wasn't hiding then."

"Don't try to get away. When we go back to the others, I want you to be one of us—body and soul. You have no reason not to. Without a license, without a plane, without money, you're back in Skid Row in a week."

"But this is my country."

She laughed bitterly. "And a lot it's done for you. Almost killed you in Italy, impounded your money, confiscated your airline, and turned you out into the street. Sure, America's great. It's great for the millionaires, great for anyone who was nursed on a platinum nipple. What have you got to be grateful for? Tell me!"

The words had come so fast, so savagely, that he could not combat them. His mind was unwilling to reject what she had said. He closed his eyes wearily. "I'm tired," he said. "Too tired to think."

She sat up beside him, her arms around his shoulders. "We pay well, darling," she said. "The Party remembers its friends."

Her words seemed to come from a distance. He said, "This is hostile to everything I've known, everything I've ever done."

She slapped his face. Twice. The pain made him open his eyes. Loudly she said, "You fool, you haven't any alternative. Either you come with us, or Heinz and Silvio will destroy you."

For a moment he said nothing. Then, "So that's how it is."

"That's how it is."

When he said nothing, she asked, "What choice have you made?"

He turned his head so that he could see her face, the eyes black and eager, the lips parted, the aquiline nostrils open like a scenting animal. "You've already told me. There is no choice."

She kissed him then, pressing her body against his, rubbing like a cat, probing his flesh with her nails. "I was right," she whispered. "Right to remember you. Right to gamble on you. Right to let myself want you again."

His lips returned a passion he did not feel. "Will we always be together?"

"Later," she said softly. "After you've proved yourself."

"Yes," he said, turning away. "Yes. There's that ahead."

Her face followed him. "But it won't be long. You'll be back in a month. Then we'll be together; work together."

"Where am I going, Nelda?"

"Dr. Loor will tell you when we get back."

"Oh, yes. The good doctor. What will I have to do?"

"It's simple. Just fly a plane."

Webb looked at the trunk of a pine tree. "I haven't a license. I'll have to take exams, spend weeks in a Link trainer."

Nelda laughed. "We haven't time for all that. Dr. Loor has all the necessary papers. All they need is your signature."

"Where did he get them?"

Nelda stubbed out her cigarette. "Never ask questions, Comrade Webb. It's enough for you to know that we have friends." She stood up and shook out her scarf. "Everywhere."

Webb got to his feet. "I wouldn't have believed it," he said slowly. "I used to hear you and Pedro talk about the war in Spain as though it were a crusade, and I used to laugh about it. Now I know you were serious. I thought it was a little ten-penny war fought by a bunch of crazy spicks over a weak-minded king, and that there wasn't anything more to it." He looked up at the sky and began to walk toward the clearing. "I see how wrong I was."

Nelda slipped her arm through his. "You were politically unsophisticated, Jake. You didn't know the issues at stake. The Party couldn't afford to have the world know."

"And it can now?"

"Perhaps. Now there are other issues."

Webb tried to close his eyes, to forget that this was reality and everything else a dream, and in a moment they were at the clearing and the car was a few yards ahead of them. Heinz was leaning against a fender looking at his watch; Gutierrez was throwing his switchblade knife into a pine tree. They watched Webb as he opened the door for Nelda. He saw them recognize the signal in her nod, and he said, "Get in, comrades. Last one in is a counterrevolutionist."

Dr. Loor was talking to him. He said, "Even before your cure began, I told Nelda that it would be better if you were a willing worker, Mr. Webb."

Jake sat in an overstuffed plastic-covered chair. He looked at the large horse face of Dr. Loor regarding him from behind the desk. "Just call me comrade," he said.

"In time, perhaps, Mr. Webb. But not now. Not just yet. I must advise you that those who believe entrance into the ranks of the Party to be easily obtained are badly misinformed."

"I've been misinformed."

"Then you will do well to rearrange your thinking." Dr. Loor removed his pince-nez and polished the lenses with a corner of his pocket handkerchief. "Only a few candidates are finally accepted, Mr. Webb. And even they must undergo constant scrutiny, even reexamination, so long as their destinies are linked with the Party."

"I wouldn't like that."

"It would depend. Yes. It would depend, Mr. Webb, on your own valuation of the goal ahead—the height you might reach within the Party edifice."

Webb nodded slowly. "I'm not precisely fired with ambition."

"Quite understandable. A reflection of your bourgeois indoctrination."

Webb shrugged. "We're creatures of environment, aren't we?"

"Unquestionably. But even environment—particularly mental milieus—can be refabricated to conform to certain requirements."

"I understand that," Webb said, "but I'm not ready for dialectical discussions."

Loor opened a drawer in his desk and took out some papers. "I am aware of your philosophical lacunae, Mr. Webb, and I will know when you are ready to engage in progressive discussion. For the meantime, your signature on these applications will suffice."

Webb got up from his chair. "Applications for what?"

"For your recertification as a commercial pilot."

Webb looked at the forms. They were neatly and completely typed. As he scanned the first page, a feeling of shock came over him that so much information concerning himself was available to people like Loor.

Loor extended a pen toward him. "Naturally they are correct in every detail."

"They would be." Webb took the pen and began signing his name. He signed it five times and gave the pen back to Loor. He said, "I suppose this gets back my license."

"Without question."

"I don't believe it."

Loor laughed, but the sound was not mirthful. "Your belief is not a necessary ingredient to success."

"If I had money, we'd have a bet."

"Unfortunately, I am still something of a sportsman and I cannot bet on a certainty." Loor folded the papers into an envelope and returned them to his desk drawer. "Besides, as you have artlessly indicated, you lack funds."

"If steak were a penny a pound, I couldn't buy a hamburger."

Loor extracted a long European wallet from his coat pocket. He held some bills between his two fingers, extending them toward Webb. "Consider this an advance against future services."

Webb took the money and stared at five one-hundred-dollar bills. "Where I come from this pays for considerable service."

"I expect it to."

Webb folded the bills into his pocket. He sat on the arm of his chair and looked at Loor. "What kind of services would you have in mind?"

"Quite obviously something connected with aircraft."

"Air Caribe?"

Loor shook his head. "Hardly that. What I have in mind is a one-time service characterized by a high degree of efficiency."

"You want me to fly." Webb did not make a question of the words.

Loor nodded. "A C-forty-six has been purchased for your use. I believe the type is familiar to you."

"I flew them for Air Caribe. Where is it?"

"Miami, Florida. You will fly it from there."

"How far?"

Loor stood up behind his desk. "You will be told when you are airborne."

Webb rose from the arm of his chair and straightened his coat. "If you won't tell me where I'm going, tell me what I'm taking."

"Certainly, Heinz and Silvio will be your crew. In the cargo compartment will be boxes and crates of importance."

"Anything else?"

Loor nodded. "You will have a passenger; an old man whose mind, unfortunately, has failed. Because of his condition he is denied more orthodox methods of egress."

"Anyone I'd know?"

Loor shook his head and took off the pince-nez. He began polishing a lens. "No. No one you might know."

"Is that all?"

"For the moment there is nothing else. Tomorrow you will leave Waverly for Miami."

Webb looked at his strengthening hands, at their new-found steadiness. He said, "Do I have a choice?"

"No," Loor said softly, "No choice at all."

Nelda flew with him to Miami. Heinz and Silvio were to join them the next day by a different route. Webb slept most of the way. A limousine took them across the Causeway to Miami Beach and deposited them at the porte-cochere of a tall hotel that gleamed with glass brick and chrome. The season had almost ended, and there was no difficulty in getting connecting rooms that faced the ocean. Webb stood in front of a mirror, trimming his new mustache, looking down five stories at the blue, leaf-shaped pool, the high white diving tower, and the placid ocean beyond.

He remembered Miami Beach in '44, jammed with black-marketeers, heavy-money boys, touts, bookies, refugees, Air Force training squadrons that marched the streets in rhythmic cadence, the sound of their singing filling the air from dawn until sunset. And now they were gone. The beach had not changed.

Webb went to the phone and ordered a ham and turkey sandwich and a quart of milk. It was late afternoon, and he was hungry. As he ate, he looked over the balcony at the sky line where the deep-sea fishing boats were heading back toward shore. An old biplane flew low over the beach, towing a curling sign that advertised a Miami restaurant near the track. From Nelda's room came the sound of a shower being turned off. Webb finished his milk, stood up, took out a package of chewing gum, and lay down on the double bed.

Closing his eyes, he could hear the soft *swish-swish* of the waves as they rolled up on the sand, then washed back into the ocean. The clean, dry scent of salt air filled his nostrils and lulled him into a kind of half sleep, and as he lay there, closing his eyes, he saw the connecting door open, and Nelda came into the room. She wore a white silk negligee with puffed sleeves, and her black hair, usually coiled, hung nearly to her waist.

She said, "Sleeping?"

"Almost."

She came toward the bed. Her negligee hid her feet, and the effect was that of effortless gliding. He said, "You look fine."

"I feel fine." She sat on the bed beside him and touched his forehead. "You look fine, too, Jake."

"In a week I'll look better. I need some sun."

Nelda shook her head slowly. "In a week you won't be here. You'll be gone."

Jake rubbed his eyes with his forearm. "I knew it was too good to last."

"Most things are. That's why only the present counts."

He looked up at her as she bent toward him. "I've heard you say that before."

"Yes. I said it to you while Pedro was alive." She let her palm rest against his cheek. "He's dead now."

Jake nodded. "Very dead. But you'd say it even if he were still alive."

"I'd say it if he were sitting in the next room."

Jake raised himself on his elbows, his arms brushing her breasts. "Nothing troubles you," he said. "Nothing haunts you. You can choose the memories you want and grind out the others."

"Of course. It's the only way life is bearable."

"Maybe I'll get that way, Nelda. Maybe I'll be able to forget everything I ever knew, even learned. But just now, I'm not ready to try."

"I'll help you," she said suddenly, and bent her head to kiss him. His arms closed around her shoulders, and he could feel her teeth rubbing his dry lips, making them moist and full. Webb lay back, drawing her with him, and said, "This could help a lot." Inside him grew a need for her that he tried to fight. He turned his head on the pillow and said, "How long do we have?"

"Tonight, my love. We're only sure of tonight."

"It's not enough." His fingers probed deep into her muscles. "When will I see you again?"

Her finger traced the outline of his lips. "When you come back. Maybe before."

"Then I'll be coming back?"

She nodded. "It's in the plan."

"Good," he said. "I figured this for a one-way trip."

"It depends on you." She started to rise, and he tried to draw her back, but she said, "Not this moment, Jake. Not quite like this. Let's make it something to remember."

"I won't have any trouble remembering."

She shook her head as she stood up, and her hair swirled around her shoulders like a dark casting net. "We'll go swimming," she said. "The way we used to when Pedro was there. Then I'll come back here, only this time I won't be with Pedro."

His flesh crawled a little, but desire thickened his voice. "I haven't a suit," he said.

Nelda went to her room and came back. She dropped a pair of swimming trunks beside Webb. "I think of everything," she said. "This is the way I want it."

Webb sat up, pulled off his shirt, and loosened his belt. Nelda went into her room and closed the door.

He was taking a towel from the bathroom when Nelda came back. She wore a swimming cap that covered her hair, a two-piece white suit that showed the vault of her thorax, her lightly muscled loins, the high uplift of her mature breasts. She touched the suit at her hips. "Like it?" she asked.

"Sure. Something new?"

"Of course. To be used once and then destroyed."

"That could run into money."

"If I did it often enough. But I don't."

Webb took her arm. "Tell me about it," he said. "Tell me about it while we're swimming."

The sun was almost down as they drifted toward the beach. They had kissed underwater, and clung together in the waves, their bodies sharing the physical punishment of the breakers. On his left, Webb could see the dark silhouette of the Roney-Plaza, the tall austere outline of the Martinique, the figure of the lifeguard walking away from the beach. He had expected that the ocean would cleanse him, that the things he did not like to think about would dissolve, leaving him buoyant. Instead, memories of Pedro and the half-lewd teasing of Nelda had choked him, until now he wanted only to run onto the beach and dry himself in the wind.

She drifted ahead of him, and he could see the symmetrical outline of her body, the small waist that widened into full, firm buttocks, the tapering thighs, and the light ripple of muscles across her bare back. The feeling came over him that in a barbaric way she was preparing him for the consummation, the way a bull is pampered and curried before the *corrida;* that she had been postponing the moment consciously in order to luxuriate in the heat of delayed desire. It came to him that in a peculiarly perverted way the woman was inflicting on him an act of psychological sadism.

He could see the small neck only a few feet away, the rhythmically expanding torso, and as he paused in the water he began to think how easy it would be to kill her. From behind he could crush her larynx with his forearm or stun her with a rabbit punch and let the water do the rest. Or he could do it the hard way, with his hands around her windpipe, and watch her eyes glaze and her tongue protrude as life left her body. But as he moved toward her, she turned unexpectedly and said, "Come on, Jake, I can't stand it any longer," and with a few strokes drew ahead of him and stood upright breast-deep in the water.

Then he knew it was no use, that he would perform his service for her, to her ultimate and final satisfaction, and that if he were ever to destroy this woman of evil, the moment was not yet come.

She ran over the sand ahead of him, in between the closed cabanas and around the curving rim of the dark pool, until they were at the hotel's beach entrance, waiting for the elevator. Both of them were breathing heavily when the door opened and a tired Negro said, "What floor, please?"

Jake said, "Six, please," and stepped to the back of the elevator, followed by Nelda. The Negro's back was toward them, and as they rose she put her arms around him, forcing her breasts against his heaving chest. Her teeth and tongue played with his ear, and her body heated his from shoulder to knee.

They walked down the hall together, and as he took out her room key from the change pocket in his trunks, she pulled off her helmet. The black hair cascaded down over her shoulders and swayed against her back. He pushed the door open into darkness relieved only by the last light of day on the rim of the ocean.

Her voice low, she said, "Don't put on the lights."

"I hadn't planned to."

She dropped the rubber helmet to the floor. "Want to take a shower?"

"Why should I? I'm wet now."

She made a little hissing laugh, and then, silhouetted against the ocean sky, she began to undo her halter.

Webb moved toward her. He said, "Stop, Nelda," and saw her arms drop to her sides.

"What's the ma—"

But his hand caught the halter in front, and with a quick jerk he ripped the light, wet fabric.

Her arms went around him then, and her voice said, "I thought we were doing this my way."

His hands fumbled with the single lace at her hip. Before he undid the knot, he said angrily, "Let's not cheat each other, Nelda. This *is* your way."

Then, as her body flowed into his, as her nails caught and tore at his back, she whispered, "Yes. This is my way. The way I planned it. The way it had to be."

CHAPTER FOUR

NELDA HAD GONE when he wakened: bags, toilet articles, and even the torn bathing suit. In his own room he showered, wincing as the soap cauterized the little cuts in his flesh.

He was eating breakfast on the balcony when there was a knock on the door. He called, "Come in," thinking the waiter would have a key, and when the knocking continued, he thought that Nelda might have come back; he got up and opened the door.

Gutierrez pushed his way into the room.

Webb turned his back and went back to the balcony. Silvio followed him to the balcony door. He sneered, "Living in style, wino?"

"It suits me." Jake took the top off a pint of milk and filled a glass. Watching Gutierrez, he drank it.

Silvio lounged against the doorframe. He took out his switch-blade knife and pressed the button, and the long, thin blade licked outward like the tongue of a snake. He held the blade carefully between two fingers and began to clean the thumbnail of his other hand.

Webb picked up the half-empty milk bottle.

Gutierrez said, "How come you ain't drinkin' wine, wino? Ain't you got no money?" He took a coin from his pocket and flipped it at Webb's feet. The coin glanced off the floor and vanished through the balcony.

Webb said, "Save your salary, pachuco. Jobs are hard to get."

Gutierrez said, "I asked you a question, wino. Where's your bottle of wine?"

Webb looked at him and said, "I like milk, pachuco. Try some." His hand launched the milk into Silvio's face; his right heel caught the man's knee, bending it the wrong way. As Silvio buckled forward, Webb twisted the knife from his hand and kneed him in the face and backward into the room. The Latin lay on his back, moaning, holding his face with his hands.

Webb knelt beside him and laid the edge of the knife across Silvio's throat. He said, "If you think the knee business was tough, pachuco, try getting up," and bore down a little with the blade. The color left the Latin's brown face. His long sideburns looked as black as undertaker's crepe. He started to say something, then his eyes rolled downward in terror as he tried to see the knife against his throat.

Webb said, "Something on your mind, pachuco? Got some more dirty cracks about my former drinking habits?"

The eyes rolled upward in supplication. Webb could feel the blood pumping through his own body. He had to restrain himself from pushing the knife into Silvio's throat. The nervous tremble of his hand sawed the knife a fraction of an inch. A thin line of blood began to well alongside the bright steel blade. It spread quickly, then dropped from the neck to Silvio's shirt collar. Webb touched the index finger of his left hand into Silvio's blood, and held it in front of the prone man's eyes.

He said, "It's your blood, pachuco. Not mine. You're smarter than Heinz, so I won't waste time telling you what I could do to you now. Since we're in this thing together, I won't do what I've been itching to do since the first time I smelled you. Use your head and figure out just how we stand now. You and I. If you think you can take me, just say so."

A sob welled up from the Latin's throat. His body twitched convulsively.

Webb laughed humorlessly. "Not talking, pachuco? Well, the big scare's over, but the next time I'll forget we're partners." He drew back the knife, put its point into the carpet, and bent the blade at an angle. The point went through the cloth until it struck bare cement and the knife began to bend. Silvio's head turned; his eyes watched the curving blade of his knife. Webb put his body's weight into the pressure, and suddenly the blade snapped. It made a sound like a broken banjo string, and the point end bounced back from the wall. Webb picked it up, carried the two pieces to the balcony, and tossed them toward the ocean. Then he looked back at Gutierrez. The Latin was holding a handkerchief against his throat, and tears of hysteria ran down his cheeks.

Webb sat down at his table and began eating a piece of cold buttered toast. The empty milk bottle lay near the door; the carpet was dark with milk splotches. He said, "Now that we understand each other, suppose you tell me what you came here to say."

Gutierrez nodded his head spasmodically. He got to his knees, and Webb said, "I didn't say to get up. I said to tell me what you had on your mind. Was it about Nelda?"

Silvio's voice was strangely cracked. It said, "No."

Webb dabbed a napkin to his lips. "What, then?"

"I was told to let you know we are here."

"You, Heinz, and the old man?"

"Yes."

"How about the plane?"

"It's ready to go."

Webb felt the old tensing of his muscles. "Who says so?"

"The CAA inspectors."

"When?"

"Yesterday."

Webb smiled. "That's more like it. Who runs the radio for me?"

"Heinz."

"And what do you do, pachuco? Smoke reefers while the rest of us work?"

"I—I guard the old man."

"That's helpful," Webb said. "You're about as necessary as breasts on a boar." He got up from the table, picked up the milk glass, and looked down at Gutierrez. "You won't bleed to death. If Heinz asks you, tell him you got a free shave at a barber college. Now get up and get out."

Gutierrez limped to the door without looking back.

Webb said, "Anything to stop me from testing the plane?"

"Heinz must go with you."

Webb laughed. "He'll love it, pachuco. You're lucky as a Mexican pig. Tell the Kraut I'll be at the airport in an hour. After a year on the ground I need practice."

The plane was in surprisingly good condition. Webb talked with the men who had reconditioned it and the pilot who had test-flown it, and made notes on its flight characteristics. Heinz sat in the copilot's seat, looking apprehensively at the control tower, as Webb ran up the engines and tested the controls. When Jake released the brakes the plane rolled forward, slowly at first, even awkwardly, until the wings began to lift and he brought the tail off the ground. He held down the nose until the last moment, then pulled the wheel back, bringing the plane up into a steep droning climb. Over Biscayne Bay he banked and slid the nose toward Bimini.

For fifteen minutes he let the plane fly itself, then he began rolling it, snapping into chandelles, laying it on its back, kicking it into a spin from which he recovered so low that he could see the face of a native fisherman on a sponge boat. When he looked at Heinz, the German's usually red face was white as a shark's belly. His chin rested on his chest and he breathed with difficulty, his eyes closed. Webb laughed and turned the plane back toward the coast, checking the rpms, the rate of climb, the automatic pilot, and the other instruments. He pushed Heinz and said, "Call the tower for landing instructions." Heinz staggered back into the radio compartment, and Webb waggled the ailerons, slamming the German against the metal side of the passageway.

Through his headphones he could hear the tower signal increase in volume, then Heinz came back to the copilot's seat. He leaned toward Webb and said, "No more funny stuff, smart boy."

Webb pointed to the cloudless sky. "Bad weather," he said. "Have to expect bumps now and then."

"Not like that one," Heinz said. "Stay dumb and we won't have no trouble."

Webb nodded solemnly. The thrill of flying again boosted his spirits the way cheap wine once had. Below him rocked a clutch of charter fishing boats, ahead was the crescent of Miami Beach. Webb called the tower and turned into the landing pattern.

When he walked out of the airport building, he noticed a man standing near the cab stand, smoking a cigarette. Heinz had left half an hour before, while Webb was getting the plane fueled and towed into a hangar. The man with the cigarette came toward Webb. He threw away the cigarette, put his hands in the pockets of his shiny plaid suit, and said, "Split a cab to town?"

"No, thanks, friend."

"Rate's pretty high, especially if you're new around here."

"I can afford it," Webb said. "One of my goats paid off at Tropical yesterday."

The man in the plaid suit shook his head. "You're luckier than I been," he said. "If you'd split the cab with me, I could save myself a buck."

"What makes you think I'm going where you want to go?"

The man shrugged. "I don't know. Something about you, maybe. Now, if you'd see things my way, I'd be glad to toss in a pint of wine."

Webb looked at him. "Just like that," he said. "A whole pint of wine. And for doing nothing at all." Something close to fear began to squirm in his belly.

The man looked down at his feet. Almost regretfully he said, "I thought you'd remember the wine."

Webb signaled a cab, opened the door, and pointed inside. “Let’s go,” he said. “The ride’s on me.”

The man in the plaid suit got into the taxi and sat in the far corner. Webb closed the cab door and looked at the man. “Well,” he said, “where do we go?”

The man coughed uncomfortably. “Somewhere quiet,” he said. “Somewhere your friends won’t likely see us talking.”

“Name it.”

“How about your room?”

“It’s as private as Market Street.”

“A bar, then.”

Webb shook his head. “I can’t handle the stuff anymore. We’ll make it a milk bar, friend. There’s one near Collins Avenue.” He gave the driver the address, and as the cab rolled away Webb looked at the outline of the man’s chest. The tight coat was buttoned over a filled shoulder holster.

The plaid man looked at his milk shake in distaste. “You’ve sure changed, mister,” he said. “You’ve sure changed.”

“What makes you think a pint of wine ever meant anything to me?”

“Two things,” the man said. “The way you grabbed at a pint I bought you in San Francisco …”

“And?”

“And the woman.”

Webb did not say anything for a moment. Then, “Why would you be buying me a pint of wine?”

“That’s easy. I was paid to. I was paid to watch you and keep you passed out on your sack.”

“Who paid you?” Webb asked, knowing the answer.

“The dame—the woman, I mean. The one who said she was your wife.”

“Who says she isn’t?”

“Uh-uh. Not when you register in different rooms.”

"You know a lot," Webb said. "The rooms were adjoining."

"Handy," the man said. "Mighty handy."

Webb swirled his milk shake with a straw. "Friend," he said, "even if what you say is true, I don't get your angle."

"The name's Ferdy," the man said. "Don't worry, I ain't a federal man. I run a not too busy eye agency—when I work. I'm small stuff, sure, but that don't mean I can't smell something big."

"How big?"

"Big enough to interest the feds. Big enough to pay my expenses and then some. Just for being patriotic."

"I see," Webb said. "Then why haven't you put the feds on the woman?"

"It was a thought," Ferdy admitted, "but there's no expense dough in a caper like that. The feds pay off on a wrapped package."

"And who would that include?"

Ferdy said, hesitantly, "The woman, Dr. Loor, the old man, and you."

Webb leaned back against his chair. "You interest me, friend," he said. "And just who might the old man be?"

Ferdy laughed. He laughed noiselessly, the grin spreading from his mouth to his ears. When he stopped laughing he said, "I guess you don't read the papers, mister. They say alky ruins the eyes."

"So I heard." Webb leaned forward across the table tensely. "The name, friend. The old man's name."

Ferdy looked around the room secretively. "If you don't know, I guess you oughta, mister. The old guy's name is Capska."

Webb relaxed. "What about it?"

"What about it? Listen. A while back—about the time I was telling you—an old guy from the UN tries to duck out on the boys back home. He nearly makes it, but someone, maybe his secretary, passes the word along, and the woman and Dr. Loor get hold of him."

"And this man was Capska?"

"Right. Only everyone thinks he's dead. They pulled a body out of the East River last week, and the Czechs all say it was Capska."

"Who do you say it was?"

Ferdy shrugged. "Some surplus stiff. What I do know is that Capska's in Miami Beach, in a room with the long-haired pachuco, and you're practicing flying in a transport airplane, so how else could it look?"

Webb lost interest in his milk shake. "Tell me about Capska."

"I only know what I read in the papers. Served in the London exile government during the war, then went back to Prague in the Czech cabinet. Stayed even after the Commies took over because the people liked him so much. He went to the UN as a delegate because he thought he could help his people—not the Commies—and then one day he turns up missing, and later they find a body." He looked at Webb. "The way I figure it, the news of his death breaks the back of any anti-Communist resistance in Czechoslovakia."

The little man's face was earnest. His hands opened and closed pleadingly. "And you're going to fly him back to the Commies so they can torture him and find out who else is against them."

Webb breathed deeply. The story had shaken him to the core. "For a private eye, you've got a pretty good grip on the world situation, friend. How come?"

Ferdy looked down at the table. "I was with Patton's army," he said. "I did CI work. If they'd let us roll into Prague, all this wouldn't have happened."

"So that's why you're interested in Czech affairs."

"That's one reason. The other is my mother came from Moravia. Her folks are still there. I don't like what the Commies are doing to the old people."

Webb said, "It's quite a story you're selling, friend. Do you think the feds will buy it?"

Ferdy looked at him evenly. "Not without you, mister. They wouldn't believe it unless you said it was so."

"How can I be sure it's the way you tell it? For instance, how do you know Capska's alive?"

"Because I was in the bushes at Waverly the night they brought him there—the night they dragged you out of the flophouse and took you to Waverly."

"If it was night, how could you see him?"

"Easy. When the car door opens, the lights go on for a minute. Then, while they're waiting on the steps, the light hits his face again."

"And you just happened to be in the bushes waiting for Capska to drive up?"

"No. I didn't know about him until I saw him. It was the woman that interested me. I figured she had a phony story about you being her husband, and I wanted to find out what I could."

Webb smiled thinly. "For future reference?"

"Yeah. I was making an investment."

Webb emptied his glass. "Drink up," he said. "Tell me what's to be done."

Ferdy pushed away the milk shake. "The woman's gone," he said. "Hell, you know that. There's only the four of you here. If the feds make the pickup, they'll make it so it happens here and on the Coast at the same time. To make it look right, they pick you up, too, and when the pay-off comes, I split with you."

"What if there isn't a pay-off?"

"Then I do business with Loor."

Webb laid a dollar bill on the table. The sad-eyed waitress stopped picking her teeth and scooped up the bill like a vacuum cleaner. Webb watched the little man's shoulders sag; a little man in a big game, Webb thought, figuring out a two-way pay-off—the kind that never comes through either way.

Webb stood up and pushed away the table. "I'm mixed up with these people," he said, "for reasons I hardly understand myself. Flying a plane is one thing, with a little smuggling tossed in for excitement, but kidnaping is a hell of a lot different."

Ferdy looked up at him. "You've got my life in your hands, mister. And you're soft on the dame. I got a bushel of worries."

Webb looked down at him. "We only sleep together," he said. "We're not really friends."

Ferdy stood up, fumbling for a cigarette. "We oughtn't to be seen together," he said, and looked at his watch. "I'll try to see a federal man now and set up the pinch."

"Anything I can do?"

Ferdy nodded. "Find out what you can about their friends and contacts here. Maybe they'll tell you the kind of plans they have for Capska on the other side."

"I'll try," Webb said. He took a hundred-dollar bill from his pocket and gave it to Ferdy. "This is for any phone calls you might have to make."

The little man pocketed the bill. "Thanks," he said. "Plane fare comes high, and I ain't worked for a few weeks. You'll get it back, mister. With interest."

"Will you be getting in touch with me?"

Ferdy shook his head. "It's better if I don't. You'll be leaving pretty quick because they won't want to keep Capska here much longer. They know the plane flies, and that's all they were waiting for. I'm kinda surprised the woman left, though." He looked at Webb. "Any reason why she shouldn't have waited?"

"None I know of."

"Well, thanks, mister, and remember, we got nothin' on them unless you talk."

"I'll talk," Webb said. "I'll hang from my tail and do tricks." He walked out of the milk bar and stood on a corner until the little man came out and turned the other way.

When he got back to his room, Heinz was sitting on a chair twirling a .38 around his index finger. He looked up at Webb and said, "You take your time, don't you?"

"A plane's a complicated piece of machinery. I want it to take us all the way."

“I called the hangar and they said you’d left.”

“I was tired. I took a walk.”

“O.K.,” Heinz said. “You took a walk.” He put the Walther automatic into his shoulder holster. “Remember to come back from your walks and we’ll get along fine.”

“Don’t worry about me, comrade,” Jake said. “I’m on a gravy train, and I know it. I’m paid to fly a plane.”

“Sure,” Heinz said. “Sure you are. And we’re leaving tomorrow.”

“That’s sooner than I’d planned on.”

“What’s wrong? The plane flies. It’s full of gas, and the sooner we get away, the fewer questions will be asked.”

Webb sat down and pulled an air chart from his pocket. “Where do I file flight clearance to?”

“Puerto Rico.”

“And where do we land?”

“We don’t land at Puerto Rico,” Heinz said. “That’s enough for you to know.”

“I have to have charts,” Webb said. “I can’t fly by the smell of the wind.”

“Buy them all,” Heinz said. “Buy them from here to Istanbul.”

“I’ll get them,” Webb said. “Now tell me when we leave.”

“We fly at night.”

“I’ll be there.”

“You sure will,” Heinz said. “Because from now on I’ll stick as close to you as a postage stamp on a letter.” Heinz stayed with him until four o’clock the next day. Jake bought air charts, flying gear, box lunches, blankets, air pillows, and thermos bottles, and loaded them aboard the plane. At five o’clock he began to wonder if Ferdy would show up, or if the feds would come aboard the plane after everyone was buttoned up. Because he did not think the plane would be flying anywhere, he found it hard to work as he should. It seemed as though he were only making a dry-run check-off, the way you did at flying school, knowing you would not actually fly for another four weeks. When the plane was towed out to the flight lines, Webb ran up the engines, tested the propellers' variable pitch, checked the radio gear and the landing lights, and switched off the engines. A fuel truck topped off his tanks again, and while the man with the hose stood on the wing, Webb sat back in his pilot's seat and closed his eyes.

A surge of recollections came to him, starting with San Francisco and Waverly, then Nelda, and finally the little man in the worn plaid suit. To Jake, it did not seem possible that he had been made part of an elaborate plan to return an unwilling diplomat to Central Europe, or that Ferdy could have learned so much so quickly. Only yesterday afternoon he had made his contact with the little man, and now, unless something happened, the plan would go through; the plane would clear Miami for San Juan, and no one would ever hear of Jaro Capska again.

True, Webb had been on the tear for a while, but the talk had been of a different game. It was one thing to act as a private pilot for a bunch of bad hats; another to conspire with the enemies of America. So far as Nelda knew, he had sold out to her, and their consummation had seemed proof of it. Undoubtedly she was back at Waverly by now, telling Dr. Loor that the plan could not fail. Webb could visualize a ring of grimfaced men, taking positions around Waverly, waiting for Nelda and Loor to come out.

Jake opened his eyes and looked toward the hangar. The gasoline truck had driven away, and there was no one near the C-46. Where were Ferdy and the men he had gone to see? Webb left the pilot's compartment and walked aft toward the door. He stood leaning his arm against the doorframe, looking down at the aluminum steps. Night was falling over the airstrip; the exhaust stacks of passing aircraft blasted streaks of red and blue into the darkness. The airport beacon flashed beams of green and red into the sky. Inside the hangar an acetylene torch flared, silhouetting a wing assembly that was being repaired, and in its sudden light Jake could see three figures walking toward the plane.

The torch flared again, and Webb saw a bulk that was Heinz. The others must be Gutierrez and Capska. As he stood at the doorway, a flashlight beam caught his eyes and Heinz called out to him, "Everything ready?"

"All set."

Heinz and Silvio half carried the old man up the steps and Webb caught a glimpse of his face, old and tired and obviously drugged; the same man he had seen at Waverly. Then they were inside the plane, leaving Webb to peer into the darkness, wondering when the federal men would come. He looked into the cabin and saw Heinz and Silvio lifting Capska onto a canvas bunk. Capska's eyes rolled in the glare of the flashlight, his body seemed to withdraw into itself, and then the eyelids closed. Heinz began strapping the body to the bunk. Gutierrez said, "That last shot you gave him put him out."

Heinz said, "It was supposed to." He finished strapping in Capska and looked back toward Webb. "Let's go," he said.

"I want another talk with Weather," Webb said. He started to walk out of the door.

Heinz pulled out his Walther and pointed it at Jake. "Forget it, smart boy. You don't know which way we're going, so it won't do you no good to ask about the weather in San Juan."

Webb came back into the cabin. He had looked toward the hangar again, in that brief moment, but saw no one in the darkness. He stepped past Silvio, who brought out a switch-blade knife and began cleaning it. Webb said, "I see you got another."

"Yeah," Heinz said. "He lost the other." Then he laughed, looked at Gutierrez, and said, "You didn't have it a day before you got a chance to use it."

"On coconuts?" Webb asked.

"No," Heinz said. "Some guy who came around looking for trouble." He looked at Gutierrez. "Silvio knifed him on general principles, and then when he frisked him, it turned out he was the same private eye Nelda hired to tail you."

Webb felt the air leave his lungs as though he had been bayoneted. “Good work,” he said. “Where’s the body?”

“I dumped it in a canal,” Silvio purred. “I burned his papers. There’s absolutely no way to tell who he was.”

“That’s using your head,” Webb said, and forced his legs to carry him toward the pilot’s compartment. “The hell with guys who meddle in what doesn’t concern them.” He felt like crying; not because Ferdy was dead, but because he had counted on Ferdy to prevent this thing from happening. For more than twenty-four hours he had let himself believe that men would be at the airport to stop the plane, to arrest them all. Now Ferdy was dead. Dead before he had talked to the federal men who should have come with drawn guns and a warrant; dead before he had told anyone of Loor’s incredible plan to return Capska to Prague. Webb coughed convulsively and pushed open the pilot’s door. His mind whirled in a montage of faces, wisps of conversations, and raking emotion. His hands moved automatically, turning on switches, adjusting levers; his eyes played over the bank of instruments in front of him and overhead. Behind him he heard the slam of the cabin door, its sound cutting through the radio static like the slap of a guillotine.

The port engine exploded into life, then the starboard. The beacon lighted the tips of the propellers, creating a silver arc in the darkness. He worked the controls lightly, then released the brakes. The big plane trundled slowly onto the paved runway, and Webb began talking to the tower.

While he was waiting for clearance, Heinz came up from the radio compartment and strapped himself into the copilot’s seat. He said, “I tell you now which way we go.”

Webb inclined his head. “Where to?”

Heinz looked at Webb, a half-smile on his putty face, and said, “Bermuda. We must reach there before it is known we have not gone to San Juan.”

It was the logical way to go. Webb had been afraid it would be by way of Recife and Dakar. He had flown before from Bermuda to the Azores and into Scotland, and the flight ahead, in a professional sense, did not bother him. It was the act of conspiracy that stabbed him like a machete, and as he sat, poised over the controls, the tower flashed green, and Webb pushed the throttles all the way forward. The racing pavement glared up in the reflection of the plane's powerful wing lights, and when the tail was off the ground, Webb pulled back gently on the wheel. The lightly loaded plane was airborne so smoothly he could not tell when the separation had been made, and then they were over the bay, with the lights of Miami in the distance.

CHAPTER FIVE

THEY REACHED Kindley Field, Bermuda, fueled, and took off again before midnight for the Azores. With a twenty-knot tail wind, Jake calculated landfall around seven. He set the automatic pilot, looked down at the running lights of a westbound steamer, and fell asleep. Heinz woke him each hour until dawn, and Jake stayed awake only long enough to alter the course, reset the autopilot, and shift fuel tanks.

At seven he had not sighted the islands, but the plane was close enough so that he got a radio fix and corrected his dead-reckoning error. While the plane was being refueled, Silvio went into the airport restaurant and brought back some box lunches. Jake ate his, looking at the dusty runway, remembering the last time he had touched down here six years before. Then, planes had come and gone at one-minute intervals and what was now a lunchroom had been a crowded pilots' mess. A small bribe cleared the plane for Casablanca, and after Webb had felt the pulse of the still sleeping Capska, he settled back into his seat, ran up the engines, and took off for French North Africa. He knew now where they were headed; over Switzerland. Although he felt that the best way to reach Prague was from Cairo, Heinz had settled the matter by showing him the itinerary, hand-written by Loor; and since Jake was supposed to be still unaware of their destination, he said nothing.

They would stop over in Bern and Heinz would make certain arrangements before flying into Prague. As he set the autopilot for

Casablanca, Webb wondered if he could find refuge for Capska in Switzerland.

Webb grounded the plane an extra three hours at Casablanca, while reluctant mechanics replaced a leaking oil line. Silvio stayed in the plane with Capska, while Heinz and Webb dozed on a pair of dusty transient pilot bunks.

They took off after dark, Jake feeling tearing fatigue in his eyes and the muscles of his back and legs, but he circled Casablanca, banking steeply so that he could see once more the town's white radiance at night, reflected back from the moon in the clear African air.

Crossing the Mediterranean, he felt once again the old feeling of familiarity as he watched for landfall on the coast of France. He check-pointed at Marseille and Grenoble and gained altitude slowly, so that when the plane passed over the Alps it was flying horizontally, its propellers biting the thinner air with increased pitch.

He called in at Bern and was told that the field at Zürich was open. Heinz looked at him and nodded. "We'll land there."

"We can go farther. We've got enough gas."

"Zürich is far enough." He picked up the phone and spoke quickly in German.

Webb wondered what had happened; why the plane was putting down in Switzerland instead of at Prague. To ask the question would let Heinz know someone had talked to Webb. Jake shrugged his shoulders. "The Swiss don't like strange planes landing at their airports," he said. "They like papers and passports and visas and flight clearances all tied up with a red, red ribbon."

"You land the plane," Heinz said. "I'll handle the red ribbons." He went back to the radio compartment, found the Zürich beam, and strapped himself into his seat again.

Webb asked, "How's the old man?"

"He's waking up," Heinz said. "Too bad I ain't got no more dope for him." He pulled a brown leather sap from his coat pocket and wagged it like a stalk of asparagus. "I guess this'll keep him quiet."

Webb looked down at the springy weapon. "That'll keep anyone quiet."

"Remember that," Heinz said. "I ain't soft like Silvio." He restored the sap to his pocket. "In a way, you done me a favor when you worked over the pachuco. I ain't had no trouble with him since."

Webb was surprised that Heinz knew of the incident. "I was lucky," he said. "He made me mad, but I probably couldn't take him again."

"Maybe not," Heinz said. "Just watch yourself after we're on the ground. Silvio didn't like the idea of you shacking up with Nelda. He's been wantin' to get into her bed for a long time."

"Tell him to jump in," Webb said. "It's a big bed with lots of room for games. He won't even have to take off his shoes." Heinz laughed and took out a cigar. He did not light it, but sat chewing the end, looking out of the convex windows at the thin drawn line on the horizon ahead.

As they were coming into the Zürich traffic pattern, Webb asked, "How long do we stay here?"

Heinz shrugged. "I make a contact in town before I find out. Just come along and don't get too curious."

Webb nodded and began preparing the plane for the letdown.

While Webb arranged for hangar space, Heinz cleared the four of them through customs and immigration. The transaction took only a few minutes, the Swiss authorities seeming satisfied with the documents Heinz produced. Webb closed his overnight bag, lifted it off the customs examination bench, and walked to the airport door with Heinz. Two men, uniformed as hospital attendants, wheeled a stretcher onto the sidewalk and loaded it into the rear of a small ambulance. Gutierrez, who had been following the stretcher, got into the rear of the ambulance and sat beside the man on the stretcher. Webb thought he heard the old man moan before the doors were closed and the ambulance drove away.

Webb looked at the rear of the departing ambulance and said, "Like Britain, Webb delivers the goods." He felt tired, suddenly, utterly exhausted mentally and physically now that the long flight was over. He wanted to lie down where he stood and sleep; sleep so that he could forget the plane in the hangar and the face of Ferdy floating somewhere in a canal, and the limp, semiconscious form of Jaro Capska.

A small boy carrying a basket of chocolates and cigarettes stopped beside Webb, and he bought chocolate bars. The effort of eating the candy kept him awake until Heinz flagged a taxi, and they rolled off toward town.

Heinz took a double room for himself and Silvio, adjoining Webb's single room. Jake was so tired he did not try to undress. He pulled the blinds against the bright morning sunlight, loosened his tie, and lay down on the bed fully clothed. A porter came into the room with fresh towels and ice water, but Webb did not hear him. He was asleep.

When he woke, it was after seven o'clock. Still groggy, he took a shower, shaved, and ordered a meal. It was served to him on heavy chinaware. The pitcher of hot milk for his powdered chocolate pleased him, and the steak, canned carrots, and mashed potatoes were quickly eaten.

He got up from the little table and looked around the barren room. For a moment it reminded him of the white-walled room at Waverly where he had been broken to Loor's needs. Then the room became a symbol of his own badly furnished life. There was nothing comfortable or permanent about the room. Its furnished-room odor was allied to that of the thousands of transient quarters he had occupied in his life. The bed was no better or worse than the median of all the beds, cots, and pool tables he had slept on since his mother and father died. A revulsion at the mediocrity and the transitoriness of his life came over him. He fingered the cheaply printed hotel stationery in the desk drawer. Even if he wanted to write a letter on such shoddy stuff, he could think of no one to whom he might reasonably write. Even if he dropped a line to Nelda, what was there to say? Thanks for an unusual lay, Nelda. Or can I pay for the torn bathing suit? Or get set for Silvio, he's got the hots for you?

Once more, as had happened other times in his life, a feeling of hollow and complete loneliness crowded every other thought from his mind. Outside, there was only the flickering of a few lights on the side of the mountain beyond the lake. A streetcar ground around a corner in the city below—the city beyond the room. He was still tired from the flight, from the change of scene and the change of emotion he had experienced during the talk with Ferdy.

Webb felt as hollow as a whore's promise.

He decided to get out of the room, even if he did nothing more than walk the streets of Zürich until he was tired enough to sleep dreamlessly again. Putting on his coat, he heard a noise at the connecting door, and as he watched the handle turn, Heinz came in.

The German said, "Going somewhere?"

"Just taking a walk."

"Where to?"

"I don't know. Name a place."

Heinz closed the door behind him and looked at the empty plates on the table. "What's the matter?" he asked. "Lonely?"

"Maybe."

"You got friends," Heinz said. "Don't start feeling lonely." He took the sap from his pocket and held it between his thumb and forefinger. He stirred it gently and the air whistled like the distant fall of a bomb. "And don't start talking to the wrong people for lack of company."

"Put it away," Webb said, turning his back to Heinz. "I've been cooped up too long. I've got to get some air."

Heinz eased the sap into his pocket. "I'll check your sack at midnight. Better be there."

Webb looked at the disarrayed bed. "I'll be back," he said. "I wouldn't want to miss a chance to see you again." Then he unlocked the hall door, pocketed the key, and went out.

At the desk he asked the clerk, "Is Mr. Gutierrez in his room?"

"I'll call."

The clerk said a few words into the phone, then turned to Webb. "Only his companion is there, Herr Kreuder. Herr Gutierrez has not yet returned."

Webb thanked him and laid ten Swiss francs on the counter. "I'm anxious to reach Herr Gutierrez," he said. "Could you tell me if he made any calls today?"

The round-faced clerk seemed to bristle. His close-cropped mustache twitched. "Moment," he said, consulted a sheet of paper, and pointed out several numbers to Webb. Jake wrote them down and thanked the clerk. He left the francs on the counter and walked out to the street. At a corner tobacco store he bought a copy of *Newsweek* and took the change to a pay phone. The first number did not answer. To the female voice answering the second, he said, in English, "Is Herr Göring there?"

"Sorry, sir," the voice said in accented English, "I do not know of any Herr Göring."

"I was to call him at this number," Webb said. "Maybe I made a mistake."

"I'm sure you did, sir. This is the Vistla Corporation."

"Thank you," Webb said politely. "Sorry I troubled you."

He hung up, deposited another coin, dialed, and heard the operator answer. In English, she told him that there was no such exchange in Zürich. She had heard of such an exchange in Bern. Should she place the call to Bern?

She should.

Webb fished out the rest of his change and waited until the operator told him to deposit it. A man's voice announced from Bern that he was speaking from the sanitarium of Herr Doktor Loor. To whom did the caller wish to speak?

"Dr. Loor," Webb said.

The man regretted that Dr. Loor was not presently in attendance. He had gone to Zürich yesterday on business, and would not return for several days. Was there a message?

In his high-school German Webb said no and thanked the man. He hung up and began eating a bar of chocolate.

So Loor was in Switzerland, in Zürich. Probably getting ready to send Capska on the last leg of the journey to Prague. On the wall beside the telephone hung a rack of maps. Webb thumbed through one until he found the outlines of Czechoslovakia, showing its relation to the Swiss border. By air, at least, Prague was not far away, three hundred miles, more or less. An hour and a half in a C-46. As he looked at the map, he realized that once he was in the air and headed east, there was no place he could land that was not under Soviet control, unless he pushed down at Munich or Linz on the pretext of engine failure. Vienna, to the southeast of Prague, was deep in the Soviet Zone, although the city and its airport were under four-power control. But a plane coming into a military airport at Munich or Linz would arouse enough interest to attract some MP's, he was sure. Then all he would have to do would be to take the MP officer aside, tell him the story, and fade out of the picture.

It felt good to think about, but when he tried it over again in his mind, the plan would not fit.

Undoubtedly Dr. Loor would be aboard the plane, armed with impressive documents that certified the charter flight to be one of medical urgency. Having seen the effect of Heinz's papers on normally curious officials, Webb decided that no MP officer would take the responsibility for holding the plane or its passengers, particularly if Loor said the patient's life would be hazarded.

He drew the paper wrapper from the end of the chocolate bar and tore it into small strips. Then he paid for the map, pocketed it, and went to the door. As he stood in the doorway wondering which way to walk, he had a sudden feeling that someone was watching him. He turned quickly, but of the three people in the shop, none seemed to have been watching him. The tobacconist was showing a carved meerschaum to a fat Swiss client, and the third man's face was hidden by a copy of the *Neue Presse.* Webb shivered a little, as though from the chill of the evening air, and walked back to the hotel.

At midnight Heinz came into the room, turned on the light, saw Webb lying awake on his bed, grunted beerily, and turned off the light.

A craving was torturing Webb; not the old frantic craving for liquor, but a new one, stronger and all-possessive. Beyond life itself he wanted someone to whom he could talk, someone who would listen while he told the almost unbelievable story of Jaro Capska's return.

The next morning he went down to the hotel's small dining room for breakfast. When the waiter took away the dishes, Webb asked, "How long has the Vistla Corporation been in Zürich?"

The waiter looked to one side, then another, surreptitiously. "I really couldn't say, sir."

Webb laid ten francs on the white tablecloth. "I've made a bet with a friend," he said. "I claim it's an old Rumanian firm that buys cuckoo clocks for export."

The waiter enveloped the francs the way a bull snake swallows a squab. His face looked cautiously interested. "And what does your friend say?"

"He says it's a Soviet firm that started here after the war. That no one knows much about it." He looked at the waiter. "Which one of us is wrong?"

"You are, sir," the waiter said blandly. He lifted the tray of dishes and walked away toward the kitchen. Webb nodded thoughtfully as he walked back to his room. Heinz was waiting for him, with Gutierrez.

Gutierrez said, "You called Bern last night, smart boy. Why?"

Webb took out a chocolate bar, peeled back the wrapper, and began eating the bittersweet chocolate. "I got lonely," he said. "When I get lonely, I call long-distance. Gives me someone to talk to. Local operators are never as smart as long-distance girls."

Gutierrez snarled and stood up. "You called Dr. Loor's place."

"Who says so?"

"The man—" Gutierrez started to say, but Heinz cut him off. "Never mind who says so. We know you done it, and I want to know why."

"You, or the Herr Doktor?"

Heinz flushed. "The Herr Doktor."

Webb remained standing. "Always be truthful, friend," he said. "If the doctor wants to know, why, so he shall. It's really quite simple when you think back to Waverly and the bronze sign that says, 'Dr. Franz Loor of Bern, Switzerland.' "

Heinz looked sideways at Silvio, then back to Webb. "So why did you call him?"

Webb shrugged. "Loor knows everything about me. I know nothing about him, and I like to know a little about the people I work for. Whether or not they're phonies, for instance. If Loor claimed to have a joint in Bern and didn't, then he showed up as a phony. Get it?"

Silvio said a four-letter word. Webb looked at him quickly. "Say it again, pachuco," he said. "Once more. Be real brave."

Silvio's face turned white and the muscles stood out along his neck. Heinz began to laugh. He made an obscene sign at

Gutierrez and simpered. "Do something, Silvio. Show us you're not a yellow-livered fairy." He leaned back on the bed, rocking with laughter.

Silvio went for his knife, but Heinz was faster. He sat upright, the Walther pointing at Silvio's stomach. The snout of the automatic gestured toward the upsprung knife in the Latin's hand. "Back," he said. "Put it back, *Schweinhund*."

When Silvio hesitated, Webb chopped the heel of his hand downward against the knife-hand wrist. The knife clattered to the floor. Webb kicked it across the rug to Heinz. Very slowly, Heinz put away the .38. He picked up the knife, released the blade, tested the edge with his thumb, and walked across the room to Gutierrez. The Latin's eyes followed him like a rabbit watching a coiling snake. Heinz put the point of the knife against Silvio's belly and called him a dirty name. Silvio's body trembled, and he began to cry. Heinz slapped his face and called him another dirty name. He pushed the knife blade back into the handle, and stuck the closed knife into Silvio's coat pocket. The Latin sank slowly to the floor and covered his face with his hands. Heinz spat at him and walked back to the bed. He sat down, took out a cigar, lighted it, and blew the smoke toward Gutierrez. Then he spoke to Webb. "No wonder they lost the war in Spain. You need men in a revolution, not fairies who want to get locked up with the prisoners."

In Spanish, he called Silvio a son of a whore, and told him to get up. The Latin staggered to his feet, eyes swollen, hair disarrayed, his body still trembling. "Get your things out of my room," Heinz said. "I'll do a lot for the Party, but I won't sleep in the same room with a fairy." He gestured toward the connecting door with his cigar, and watched Gutierrez walk around the bed and open the door. Then he laughed unpleasantly. "Don't let me catch you with a man in your room," he said, "or they'll fish you out of the Zürichsee smelling like a month-old cod."

Gutierrez closed the door behind him, and Heinz blew a smoke ring. "He's like a dago," he said. "The Italians were all fairies.

When we'd find them in bed together in the Western Desert at high noon, they'd say they was only snuggling up to get warm."

Webb took another bite from his chocolate bar. "Such a lot of memories," he said, "and all of them unpleasant." He listened to the sound of Gutierrez packing in the next room. "You've been mean to the boy," he said. "Plain mean."

Heinz scowled. "He almost got a slug in the belly. Next time, I'll gouge out his eyes and suck them like grapes." When he got up from the bed, Webb sat down on it and took off his shoes.

Heinz said, "Why ain't you takin' care of the plane?"

Webb smiled. "It's full grown," he said. "It takes care of itself now."

Heinz moved toward the hall door. "Just make sure," he said. "We could leave here any time."

Webb turned on his side and closed his eyes. "I can't wait," he said. "What do we do next? Smuggle butter into Belgium?"

The door of his room slammed shut. Webb opened his eyes and looked at the wall. That had been a close one, letting them know he had telephoned Bern, but they had turned on each other and forgotten about him. He wondered how long it would be before he had only Heinz to deal with. Thinking of flying again made him sleepy. He closed his eyes and listened to the wavering voice of an old woman selling flowers on the street below.

The sound of a zipper being opened woke him. At first it had sounded like a file rasping the leg of a chair, but when his subconscious mind recognized it for what it was, he opened his eyes. Slowly.

Facing him stood a man, closing Webb's overnight bag with one gloved hand. The other held a pistol with a long, thick barrel. Webb could see the pistol's small bore: .22 caliber, or less. He looked up, along the pistol arm, to the shoulder, then to the face. What he saw surprised him. The man's features were utterly commonplace. As much of the hair as showed under the hat was well-groomed and the man's suit was well fitting, according to British standards. Through rimless glasses, the man's eyes expressed polite interest, and his mouth moved. "Hello, laddie," it said. "This makes it awkward."

Webb raised himself on his elbows. "How true, friend," he said. "Awkward is the word."

The man's eyes lost their appearance of politeness. He sat down facing Webb and rested the pistol barrel on the back of the chair. One eye sighted along the barrel pointed at Webb's throat.

Webb asked, "Why my throat?"

In a bored professorial tone, the man said, "When the voice box is crushed, no further sound is made. With even a fatal head wound you might yelp indefinitely."

Webb laughed. "I suppose the pistol doesn't make any noise."

"No," the man said. "It doesn't." He showed it in profile to Webb. "It works on carbon dioxide. It kills with only a whisper." Without seeming to sight, the man pulled the trigger. A sound like a sigh escaped the barrel, and Webb turned his head to look at the wall. A small black hole had appeared six inches over his head. Webb looked back at the man on the chair. "Fine," he said. "I'll buy it. With a suitcase full of those I can paddle up the Amazon and make my fortune among unknown and exotic tribes." He sat up the rest of the way, put his feet on the floor, and reached for his shoes.

The man said, "This could be an extremely pleasant interview, laddie, but I'm frightfully badgered for time. In a phrase, where are they?"

"The Kraut and his friend?"

"Among others, yes."

Webb pointed to the connecting door.

The man shook his head. "Gone," he said. "Or did you know?"

Webb looked at his watch. It was after one. "I've been asleep since ten. They were here just before then." He found a shoe and began tying the lace.

The man with the pistol said, "You're taking this rather well, laddie; or was it part of the plan to leave you behind?"

Webb looked up at him. "It must have been part of the plan," he said. "Only I didn't learn about it until just now."

The pistol barrel receded from view. Webb put on his other shoe and walked to the washbasin. He splashed cold water on his face, tied his tie, and combed his hair. Then he smoothed his mustache and turned to the man again. "I'm sorry they got away," he said. "I hadn't meant them to."

"And Capska?"

Webb shrugged. "I haven't seen him since the ambulance door closed."

The man swore. "You're a queer case, laddie. You're in it with the rest of them, and yet you don't seem to care that they've gone."

Webb put on his coat. "I had a plan. I figured it out last night, but they were too fast for me.

"You flew Capska here from America?"

Webb nodded.

"It doesn't add, laddie. You were with them, now you're not."

"That's right," Webb said. "On your day off, I'll tell you the story. What's important now is what they've done with old Capska."

The man pocketed his pistol. "You're a Yank," he said, "so I'm sure you're loony. My name is Horace L. Frean." He took out his wallet, extracted a card, and handed it to Webb. He said, "If you don't read German, it says I'm the proprietor of a greeting-card and gift shop here in Zürich."

"Bully for you," Webb said. "How's business?"

"Good enough to keep me here for thirty years."

"I wonder," Webb said. "Not selling gifts like the plinker you covered me with."

"No matter, laddie. The point is, the birds have flown. It was not until last night that I realized who the patient was who came off your plane. Since then, I've wasted the time of two energetic young men by having them watch the doors of your plane's hangar." He shook his head disgustedly. "So while I watched the west, they hared away to the east."

Webb put his hands in his pockets. "You have more than a casual interest in this business."

"Rather," Frean said. "One might almost term it official."

"Where do we go from here?"

"I'm not sure," Frean said, "but I'll take a chance on you. If you've done something you've had cause to regret, I'll give you a chance to even out."

"You won't be sorry," Webb said. "I suppose the first thing is to get me out of the hotel."

"Right."

"And what's to keep me from leaving Zürich—getting out of Switzerland?"

"Have a passport?"

"No."

"Anything resembling one?"

"No."

Frean sighed. "Well, we'll take care of that. I noticed as I came up that there is a note in your box at the desk below. Probably instructions from your departed friends. I suggest that at a discreet interval after my departure you take possession of the note and come with it to my shop." He looked evenly at Webb. "By a circuitous route."

"Roger."

"And if you're thinking of getting in touch with anyone, dismiss the thought. You'll be watched from the moment you leave the hotel."

Webb laughed and pointed to the phone. Horace Frean shook his head. "The telephone operator and I are old, old friends."

"You take precautions."

"I am forced to. The lives of a great many people depend upon what I will divulge to you this afternoon—and upon your future actions." He looked out of the window, squinting at the sunlight. "Jaro Capska was a disciple of Thomas Masaryk. Both of them were friends of Britain and of the entire Free World. So long as Capska lives in freedom, hope will not die in Czechoslovakia." He looked back at Webb. "If the enemies of freedom destroy what Capska has built, then destroy him as a man—the way they destroyed Stepinac and Mindszenty—then they will have destroyed more than they have yet accomplished with all their torture, their executions, and their slave-labor camps." He looked down at Webb's overnight bag, picked it up, and handed it to him. "You've made a choice."

"It wasn't difficult."

"Like the other side, I prefer volunteers," Horace Frean said, "but having made your choice, you're committed to it. If you try to turn back, for any reason, I'll kill you myself, and laugh as your life bubbles out of your stomach."

"Understood," Webb said simply. He watched Frean go out of the door, and then he began to count the minutes on his watch. He felt breathless and a little afraid, as though he were about to test a new type of parachute. He knew that he must go through with it, but the ground was a long way away.

When Frean had been gone for twelve minutes, Webb went out of the door and walked down to the desk. He took an envelope addressed to himself from the clerk and went out to the sidewalk. As he walked in the warm afternoon, he sensed again the feeling that had come over him last night at the tobacco shop. Someone was watching him, he was sure, but this time he did not turn to see who it might be.

This time he knew.

CHAPTER SIX

ONLY OCCASIONALLY in a lifetime do you meet a man under alien circumstances whose pose is insignificant compared to the solid inner substance; whose force can assert itself without labels, uniforms, or medals. To Webb, the bland-faced Horace Frean was such a man. Even before Webb saw him standing behind a case of hand-decorated Swiss greeting cards, Webb had visualized the way he would look, and the guess had been accurate.

When Webb entered the shop, a little bell tinkled overhead and Horace Frean looked up from the gifts he was showing an elderly Belgian lady. Webb saw the polite slightly servile expression on Horace Frean's face, and turned away to keep from smiling. It seemed incredible that this stock British commercial type who had sighted a Webley air pistol at Webb's throat was now exchanging pleasantries with a foreign customer.

The Belgian lady selected two dozen cards and paid for them, and while Horace Frean wrapped her purchase, he said in a clear voice to Webb, "Please wait, sir. I'll be free in half a minute."

Bowing the lady to the door, Frean was the soul of salesmanship, the model of everything a floorwalker or complaint manager should be. Yet Webb knew that Horace Frean's real reason for existence had nothing to do with the sale of greeting cards to tourists, or with anything but the demanding and intricate game of which Webb now knew him to be a player.

Murmuring a polite good-by, Frean closed the door of the shop and turned to Webb. "Were you followed?" he asked quietly.

"No. At least, I saw no one."

"A wise answer," Horace Frean said. He stood in front of a display case, his whole manner changed from one of mercantile servility to a precise and efficient bearing that seemed almost military.

Webb looked at the piles of neatly stacked cards. "Sell many?" he said.

"Enough to keep the Swiss satisfied that the business is legitimate."

"Are you the owner?"

"No. Swiss law prevents it. I am, instead, a minority partner."

"You like Switzerland?"

Something akin to a distant smile moved Horace Frean's face. "I've found it interesting."

"For thirty years?"

"Why not? From this little shop I've seen the ashes of one war grow cold and watched the spontaneous combustion of another. And during the war against the Nazis we had some high moments here, laddie."

"Now you're watching the beginning of a third."

Frean looked past him, out of the window. "I pray that may not be the case."

"But it looks that way," Webb persisted.

Horace Frean nodded slowly. "If the echoes that reach this little listening post mean anything, it indeed looks that way."

Webb dug a small bar of bitter chocolate out of his pocket, peeled away the wrapper, and began eating it. He said, "And how does that leave me?"

Evenly, Horace Frean said, "It leaves you with a part to play, Mr. Webb. One that could be rather significant."

"You'd trust me?"

"I might."

"Why?"

Horace Frean hesitated for a moment. Then he said, "Your two friends were plotting to kill you."

"I'm not surprised, but how did you know?"

"They talked about it when they were drunk," Horace Frean said. "One of my people overhead them."

"What sharp ears you have!" Webb said.

Horace Frean took a stubby, blackened pipe from his breast pocket, filled it deftly, and lighted the tobacco. "Two men are missing, Mr. Webb. Two men of international importance."

Webb nodded. "Capska is one. Could I be the other?"

"Not this time, laddie. But the second, like yourself, is an American."

"Anyone I'd know?"

"If I told you his name, yes. But for now, I'll use the name he is known by within the Party in Moscow and Prague: Kaspar. Just Kaspar."

"Does anyone know he is missing?"

"The Party does," Frean said. "So far, the Americans have not commented officially on his absence."

"Why would there be an official comment?"

"Because he holds a quasi-official position within your government. He is sufficiently prominent within the world of American industry to merit entree at the White House, and an advisory position with half a dozen of your alphabetical agencies."

Webb whistled. "As high up as that."

Frean nodded. "His background has been questioned occasionally, but each time the matter is brought up, groups of so-called American liberals defend him so frantically that in recent months to voice suspicion concerning Kaspar's good faith arouses the same scorn that faces a cultist who ventures to establish the earth as being nonglobal in shape."

"And you won't tell me his name?"

"In a moment, my friend. I must judge your reaction before I hazard thinner ice." Horace Frean looked piercingly at Webb.

"For the sake of discussion, let us say that in spite of his monumental undercover work for the Party, Kaspar fell out of favor and was summoned to do penance—a disciplining he has refused to submit to until recently, when he realized that the mountain would have to come to Moscow—by way of Zürich."

"Why Zürich?"

"Because Zürich is the center of the purchasing and trade activities of the Soviet government."

"Openly?"

"They make little attempt to hide it. Their firm, the Vistla Corporation, buys every manner of proscribed merchandise and transships it to the East."

"I called Vistla the other night," Webb said. "I was—"

Horace Frean held up his hand. "We possess a high-fidelity recording of the conversation," he said. "It was that which made me wonder how deeply you had been converted."

"I should have thought of that."

"No matter, laddie. In addition to the normal materials of war, such as electronic devices, ball bearings, metals, and fuel, the Vistla Corporation has a consuming interest in purchasing deep-level mining equipment."

"For coal?"

Horace Frean wagged his pipe. "No. For uranium."

"I see," Webb said. He felt a little sick. "I knew they mined the stuff back of the Urals. Is that where the equipment goes?"

"It hasn't to travel very far," Frean said. "It only goes to the Erz Gebirge—the Ore Mountains."

"Germany?"

Horace Frean nodded. "On the border between Germany and Czechoslovakia. Some of the biggest uranium workings are at Karlsbad. There are others at Jáchy-mov. Both were world-famous radium spas." He knocked a layer of ashes from his pipe. "They've been closed for months even to Czechs and Germans."

"And how does Kaspar fit in?"

"We're not quite sure," Frean said, relighting his pipe. "We think he's been getting material taken off the American proscribed list, so that it could be more easily obtained for shipment to the East. But mining equipment is still under East-West sanctions."

"And you think he might try to get the ban lifted?"

"I think he might," Frean said, and looked closely at Webb. "I've compared notes with the Dutch, and they agree. The French can't make up their minds, but no matter. If Kaspar could have had the Vistla people tell him at firsthand how desperately this mining equipment was needed, he would have been in a good bargaining position by the time he reached Moscow."

"It lines up," Webb said. "But the way you tell it, Kaspar didn't get around to it."

"Quite so, laddie. Nor will he ever. By the time Kaspar had been four hours in Zürich he was irrevocably dead."

"Natural?"

"Hardly. Kaspar was a comparatively young man, in the best of health. The explanation for the premature failure of his vital processes is poison."

"Poison?"

"Administered in a whisky and soda while we drank together."

"You don't look like a poisoner," Webb said. "You don't look like a killer at all. You look like someone's father. Maybe mine."

Horace Frean's pipe had gone dead. He knocked out the ashes into a gift tray and returned the pipe to his breast pocket. "I *was* someone's father," he said. "But only until 1944. The Russians shot down my boy one night when he was dropping food and ammunition into Warsaw for General Bor's army. They said the Germans had done it, but one of the chaps who got back proved it on a chart."

Webb said nothing. There was nothing he could say without seeming either juvenile or mawkish.

Frean spoke again, slowly and with a certain dullness to his voice. “If I do not hesitate to destroy traitors, one could say that I have my own reasons.”

“Yes,” Webb said. “One could say that.” He got up from his chair and walked toward Frean. “Now that you’ve given me the build-up, give me the pitch. Kaspar’s dead, I’m here, and Capska is probably confessing while a tape recorder takes down every word.”

“It is a possibility we must face,” Frean said. “What would you suggest?”

“Get him back before it’s too late.”

“Ah, yes, laddie,” Frean said. “Just like that. We get him back, you and I, and that’s an end to it. Eh?”

Webb said, “You don’t seem to care whether he comes or goes, but I do.”

Coolly Frean said, “And so you should, my lad, since it was you who got him where he is.”

“I was the guy who flew the plane, yes. But it could have been anyone else. The Party can get men, you know. The Capska operation didn’t depend on me.”

“Then why were you recruited?”

“There was a personal angle. A woman I used to know works close to Dr. Loor.”

“Señora Ramos?”

“Yes.”

“A devotee,” Frean said. “One of the inner few. Loor uses her, they say, in order to assure success. In a way, a compliment to you.”

“So what about Capska?”

“Not an uncomplicated venture,” Frean said. “Money and lives will have to be risked. And then, even if the venture succeeds, we might find ourselves with a cow already milked dry.”

“It’s a chance to be taken.”

“By whom? By whom, dear laddie?”

"By myself," Webb almost shouted. "That's what you wanted me to say, isn't it?" His hands were shaking, his face felt flushed. He wanted to slap the bland, impervious face of Horace Frean. Then, quite unexpectedly, Frean's arm was around his shoulders, patting him in a comradely way. In its surprisingly authoritative tone, Frean's voice said, "It's *exactly* what I wanted you to say."

Webb's body relaxed so quickly that he almost gasped for air. "I'll do it," he said. "Tell me how it's to be done, and I'll do it."

Frean left him, locked the shop door, and opened the door that led upstairs and pointed toward it. "The people on our side have notoriously bad luck in what is called obtaining the breaks. The Devil seems to aid the wicked in every way. However, since the late and unlamented Comrade Kaspar was personally unknown to all except a few top Party members—and most of those in the Kremlin—his passport and other documents may serve to make the credulous believe that you are not an American pilot named Webb, but Kaspar, an underground Party member on a mission to Moscow." He smiled slightly. "By way of Prague, of course."

"Of course," Webb said. They went upstairs together. Sitting in a deep leather chair, drinking milk and reading the contents of an expensive pigskin brief case, Webb could hardly believe the name on the passport that Horace Frean said had been Kaspar's. The name was Horton S. Palmer, a man who had exemplified the rags-to-riches rise so dear to those of the Horatio Alger persuasion. Born only three years before Jake, Horton Palmer had won a newsboy's scholarship to Harvard, taken an advanced degree in business administration, and become during the war the country's most sought-after consultant on industrial management. Webb could remember reading articles written by Palmer for some of the biggest magazines in America, stating the case for internationalism and the economic necessity of trade with the Russian orbit. Palmer's position had been that of a practical American businessman who saw a vast consumer potential in the Russian sphere, and proposed that if America were willing to let

Stalin run his third of the globe as he saw fit, the broadened trade would react to the immense benefit of every American citizen.

The brief case contained fragmentary notes written by Palmer, evidently for a report or a magazine article. Webb studied them intently until he knew Palmer's position on land reclamation in Italy, nationalization of steel in Britain, and the peculiar balance-of-payments problem posed by the success of the Benelux Customs Union. Webb found himself fascinated by the workings of the dead man's mind, the ability it had possessed to peer into good and pronounce it evil. Perhaps the notes would have been framed eventually into a series of propaganda attitudes that would have been reflected eventually in every Communist-controlled organ in the world. Yes, the notes were a form of intellectual poison that tainted, suborned, and destroyed those whose minds were less alert, less devious than Palmer's.

Webb put aside Palmer's papers and let his mind work on the suggestion that Horace Frean had made regarding Palmer's influence. For instance, he thought, if Palmer had been told by the Party that Russia needed transformers badly for a new atomic pile in Rumania, and transformers happened to be on the West's proscribed list, a man in Palmer's position could ridicule the embargo on transformers by saying how fantastic it was to think that highly industralized Russia had need of an item so trivial as a transformer. The spread of innuendo would result in the embargo's being lifted, and the Vistla Corporation could purchase transformers in Schenectady, Detroit, Trieste, and Rotterdam for transshipment to the nuclear-fission site in Rumania.

A man like that, Webb realized, was more dangerous than a thousand industrial saboteurs at large in America. He had not liked the idea of poison, but now that he had read Palmer's notes and convinced himself that Palmer had been a smirking traitor, the thought of poison no longer bothered him. He did not propose to let Horace Frean know that he had changed his mind about Palmer's destruction. He was glad that Palmer's notes would never be read by an admiring American public, or that they would never find their way to the Party's committees to be read in clandestine hideaways.

Frean came back into the study, carrying Palmer's passport, and said, "I've turned Kaspar's picture inside out, and I can't think of any way to make your features resemble his. The best I can do is to make you look less like yourself, photograph you, and reattach the picture to the passport." He tossed the passport into Webb's lap, and Jake opened it to look at Palmer's photograph.

While he was looking at the face of Palmer, he heard Frean say, "How long have you worn a mustache?"

"Only a couple of months."

"Then old friends wouldn't recognize it."

"I don't think so."

"How about your weight?"

"I could use a few more pounds."

"Kaspar was heavier than you, but his clothes should fit. If they appear a trifle full in cut, no one in Europe will notice." He looked at Webb and raised his hands in a mercantile gesture. "Fashion died in 1939."

"I wouldn't know. Balmain hasn't designed for me in just ages."

Horace Frean laughed. "You'll do, lad. Now tell me, do you care if I change your hair styling?"

"I won't let you bleach it, if that's what you mean."

"No. Part it on the other side and lower your sideburns."

"O.K."

"It makes a difference, really. A tremendous difference. You see, the average person notices only what he is accustomed to see. As Jake Webb, you could reasonably be recognized by certain members of the Party, but with certain alterations in your appearance, plus the powerful documentation you will be given, you will very likely pass as Kaspar."

"And if the disguise doesn't fool anyone?"

"Then please conduct yourself so that you cannot be forced to talk. You must always remember that such facilities as we presently have behind the iron curtain have been built and maintained at a terrible cost in lives and money. To betray the secrets you will be given would be monstrous."

"I get it," Webb said dryly. "All right; they won't be able to make me talk. I'll take a dive."

In a friendly voice Frean said, "I am sorry to mention this requirement, but it is basic to our understanding."

"It's understood." Webb pointed to Kaspar's brief case. "I've read everything you gave me. What next?"

"Do you know Kaspar's vital statistics?"

Webb nodded. "Born at Chelsea, Massachusetts, on August, third, 1912. Father, Samuel Ward Palmer; mother, Sara Ellen Horton. One sister, Grace Ellen, now married to John Phillip Reber, living in Yuma, Arizona."

"Wife?"

"Josephine Adele Brinker. We met in Tuckahoe, New York, and were married in Redding, Connecticut, February seventeenth, 1941."

"Children?"

"Horton S. Palmer, Jr., student at the Pelham Country Day School."

"Mistress?"

"A social-service worker named Edna Adler who lives at Twelve Bank Street, Greenwich Village. She was a graduate of C.C.N.Y. and the New School. She was recruited into the C.C.N.Y. cell during her sophomore year."

"And when did you become a Party member?"

"When I was sixteen," Webb said. "I paid my first dues to the Charlestown cell."

"Why did you become a Communist?"

"It was a natural evolution," Webb answered. "My father had been a covert organizer of the I.W.W., and participated in the Boston streetcar strike. During the strike my family went hungry and my father was beaten by the clubs of Cossack police. One of the infuriated bourgeoisie threw a brick at my father, which broke three of his ribs and resulted, eventually, in his death."

"But the intellectual reasons?"

"They, of course, were the stronger. On the one side I had been a lifelong witness to social injustice and the exploitation of workers; on the other, to the sight of the capitalist dragon cannibalistically destroying itself by permitting the means of production to rest in the hands of a few czars of vested privilege who were using the rightful possessions of the people for self-aggrandizement."

"How often have you been paid for your work?"

"Once a month a deposit has been made in a false name in the Bowery Savings Bank."

"You can give other details?"

"If necessary."

"The number of your card?"

"I have never held a Party card. The number assigned to me under another name was seven-four-six-nine."

Horace Frean said, "That's quite enough, Kaspar. If the Party questions you more closely than that, you'd best start making other plans. If you attract that much suspicion, there is no way on earth you can lay it to rest. Functionaries usually lack depth of imagination, but if they were sufficiently suspicious, they would not hesitate to confront you with someone who had known Kaspar, or who was supposed to have known him. Remember that; don't automatically say you know someone simply because the question has been put to you in a leading way."

"No."

"Documents aren't enough by themselves. You'll have to act the part, you know—irritable at the stupidity of minor Party officials; reluctant to mention the names of others in the underground cell."

"Right."

Horace Frean leaned back in his chair and looked up at the ceiling. "One never knows when a man is ready to go," he said. "Part of it is intuition. You could read more material by and concerning Kaspar, but after the saturation point had been reached, you'd grow stale. You'd realize with a sick feeling how impossible it is to know and account for the every move of a man who lived longer than yourself, and whom you are attempting to impersonate."

"It's occurred to me."

"Then get it out of your mind. Think back to your own wartime experiences, when the CID might have arrested you for speeding, found you had left your identity card back at the barracks, and started to interrogate you. You always passed the examination, didn't you?"

"In similar cases, yes."

"And don't forget that subconsciously, every interrogator *wants* you to be whom you appear to be. No interrogator really wants to find out that you've been at hare and hounds with him and his friends."

"I'll remember that."

"I'm not trying to frighten you, laddie, but I've told these things before to a good many chaps in my work, and often enough they've had occasion to remember them."

"I'll remember."

"Good. Let's drink to it." Frean got up, walked to a cabinet, and took out a bottle of Scotch.

Webb laughed. "I don't use it any more."

"Hot chocolate then?" Frean said.

"Fine."

Frean rang for a maid, gave an order, and poured himself a shot of whisky. While they were waiting for the maid to return,

Frean went through the brief case, extracted certain papers, left the remainder inside, and closed the case.

Webb asked, "Aren't you going to take out the notes?"

"No."

"Why not? They're valuable, aren't they?"

"They're more valuable to you than anyone else. If they want you to write more, why, you can sprain your thumb."

"Am I to talk to Vistla before I go?"

"No. Dr. Loor might drop by."

"Isn't there a good chance I'll run into him before I get back with Capska?"

"I don't think so. Loor is a physician; a nerve specialist with two Sanitariums to maintain—neither of which is anywhere behind the curtain. He would have no normal reason to be going where you will go. If a strong reason should arise and Loor were to go or be sent for, it's a chance we can't anticipate."

The maid came with a pitcher of hot chocolate for Webb and a small pitcher of water for Frean. Frean poured part of the water into his whisky glass, while Webb filled a cup with hot chocolate. While they were drinking, Frean said, "About your nose."

"What about it?"

"It's too commonplace. It's straight and highly American."

"Kaspar's an American."

Frean nodded. "That's fine so long as you're Kaspar," he said. "But if you wanted to become someone else, the nose would be a difficulty."

"I'm sorry to hear about it," Webb said. "It's been broken a few times; maybe I shouldn't have bothered to have it set."

Frean did not appear to have heard him. He said, "Even the fastest operation, done tonight, would leave your nose blue and ugly for two weeks. With or without sticking plaster, you'd be more noticeable than we can afford."

"Two weeks is too long."

"Decidedly." He looked at Webb with something of a smile around his mouth. "It's a rotten shame, really, for your nose would be a joy to work with."

"Paraffin? Bone scraping?"

Frean waved his hand. "Ancient stuff. We use plastic now. Real plastic. Paraffin melts and runs. We smash the nose, pump in some plastic until the nose starts to bulge where we want it to, and let it set for two hours. When the bones knit, they knit the way the plastic forces them to."

"And the plastic?"

"It stays. Closer than mother love."

"So sorry," Webb said dryly. "Hate to spoil your fun."

Frean finished his drink, took a map from a drawer, and laid it open on top of a table. He motioned Webb to come to him. "Thank God you can read a map," he said. "No end of chaps have got themselves caught because they couldn't really read a map or forgot how when the hounds were behind them." He pointed to Zürich and said, "We start from here—figuratively speaking, of course. Your point of departure is Zürich."

"Bueno."

"You speak Spanish?"

"Enough," Webb said. "I worked in Puerto Rico."

"Another break," Horace Frean said happily. "That gives you a common language with Capska. When he was a young man, he served in Buenos Aires as a vice-consul."

"If things work out, we won't have time to talk."

"No. 'Hello,' 'Come along,' and 'Good-by.' "

"I can say all of that," Webb said. "Maybe more."

"You've got other things to think about," Frean said. "You have an address and a name to commit to memory."

"Say on."

"Very well. Seventy-three Tesnov."

"Seventy-three Tesnov," Webb repeated.

"It's across the street from the Ministry of Food."

"I'll stop by when I'm hungry."

"You'll stop by as soon as you can shake the STB."

"Secret Police?"

Frean nodded slowly. "They ape their masters, the MVD. And even the Gestapo learned its horrors from the CHEKA."

"I've heard of them," Webb said. "They worked for the czars."

"Cruelty begets cruelty. It's the Slavic tradition—the tradition of Genghis Khan."

Webb waited a moment for Frean to continue, but when he did not, Webb asked, "Where are they holding Capska?"

"Probably Hradcany Castle, but that's not confirmed yet."

"And what do I do at Seventy-three Tesnov?"

Frean began filling his pipe, squinting past Webb at the dying sun. "In a discreet fashion, you will arrange to talk with Herta Sebok. She may not be there when you arrive, and it may take a few days for your message to reach her."

"When she comes, how will I know her?"

"In Prague there is a famous clock in the square of the Old Town, built by Hanus in 1490—before America had been discovered. The dial divides the day into twenty-four hours and records the positions of the planets and the phases of the moon. Underneath the dial is an allegorical calendar of the months and the zodiac. As the hours strike, figures on the façade above the clock come to life: A skeleton wags its head, Judas rattles his moneybags, windows open, and the figures of Christ and the twelve apostles walk past. As the last figure disappears, the windows close and the cock above gives a parting crow."

"I've never heard of it before," Webb said. "It must be quite a clock."

"You shall see for yourself, laddie. Postcard pictures of the Judas clock are sold everywhere in Prague. Buy one and carry it with you. When someone comes to you saying that she is Herta Sebok, show her this picture of the clock and say, 'Which is the Judas hour?' "

“And what will she reply?”

“If she is the one you seek, she will say, ‘For each man, the hour is different; and you will say, ‘It matters not the hour, but the man.’ ”

When the words had gripped him, Webb did not say anything. Instead, he watched the sudden glow of Frean’s match lighting the blackened brier. The sun had disappeared behind a mountain peak and into the room came the chill of nightfall.

CHAPTER SEVEN

He sat in a first-class *wagon-lit* compartment, drinking a glass of iced Vichy water, looking through the dirty double panes at the lights of Munich receding in the distance. Kaspar's brief case rested on the seat beside him; in his pocket was Kaspar's wallet, filled with fifty-dollar bills, West marks, and Czech koruny. His hand touched his breast pocket and felt the American passport with its cleverly replaced photograph, its Czech visa and Russian *carte-grise.*

Already, quietly efficient men had examined his credentials, compared the passport photograph with his face, stamped cachets inside the passport, and moved on to the next compartment. Some American MP's were riding the train now, and Webb knew that later a detachment of Russian soldiers and security police would board the train to stay until he got off at Prague.

At first, he had suggested to Horace Frean that he fly into Prague, but the little Britisher had vetoed it, pointing out that train passengers attracted less attention than those who arrived at airports in small groups, and besides, it was known that Kaspar had planned to travel from Zürich by train. To Webb, it did not seem possible that he had only encountered Horace Frean two days before, so jammed had the hours been since their partnership began. He had studied commercial maps of the Zürich-Prague-Vienna triangle, learned something of the organization of Gottwald's government, and memorized the Communist careers of Vice Premier Zdenek Fierlinger, Prime Minister Antonin Zapotocky, General Prochazka, and Education

Minister Nejedly. Low types, he had thought; cowards and opportunists who spent the war years safe in London or attending quisling schools in Moscow instead of sharing the hazards of Czech resistance with their countrymen. But as he had read on, he realized that here were not Czechs of the Masaryk-Benes tradition, but countryless internationalists whose only loyalty was to the slave banner of communism. At first it had been hard to think of Kaspar as such a man, but then the realization came that had a coup occurred in America during Kaspar's life, he could easily have been another Fierlinger or Gottwald, and Webb had felt a grim joy that Horace Frean had liquidated him so fittingly in the Communist tradition.

He looked at the reflection of his face on the window glass, at the half-strange alteration in his appearance—the changed part in his hair, the thick mustache that widened his face—and wondered how long it would be before a shout went up that he was not Kaspar but an enemy to be tortured and killed. Webb drank again from his glass and shivered a little. He did not think himself either more or less brave than the average American, but the unreal situation into which he had placed himself wore on his nerves. Impersonation, deceit, and violence were contrary to every teaching he had ever absorbed, yet the gnawing shame of his collaboration with Nelda was so great that he had committed himself irrevocably to an attempt at righting the wrong he had done.

The door of his compartment slid open suddenly, and Webb turned quickly, half expecting to see a Russian soldier or a swarthy civilian with a Tokarev pistol, but it was only the waiter asking if he desired another bottle of Vichy before the dining car closed. Webb shook his head and watched the waiter slide back the door and walk down the corridor.

Alone again, Webb felt the sweat on his palms, the unnatural tenseness of his face. He finished his drink quickly and rang for the attendant to make up his berth.

Before he fell asleep he put his passport under his pillow beside a pencil flashlight, ready for the border examination.

When he woke the train had stopped and he could hear the heavy clump of boots in the passageway crossing the carpet in front of his door; the bleak piercing scream of the engine's whistle breaking through the night like the enraged neigh of a tethered and frightened horse; the pounding of fists on compartment doors; the confused murmur of voices speaking in unfamiliar languages.

Webb rang for the attendant, and when he finally came, Webb asked, "Is this the border?"

"No, sir." The attendant rubbed his hands nervously and looked over his shoulder.

"Then what is it?"

"Something else, I think." In the berth light, his face looked old and worried.

"What?"

The attendant looked around again, then bent close to Webb's face. "They say saboteurs."

"Saboteurs? What happened?"

"A log across the rails," the attendant said in a low voice, "but please not to repeat."

"Thanks," Webb said, and gave the attendant a tip.

Gratefully the attendant left, and Webb turned off the light. In the distance he could hear the shouts of voices, and after they had died away the train started with a jerk and slowly gained speed as it fought the incline of the Bohmerwald.

It was still dark when he was wakened by the attendant and two men in uniform. The attendant said, "Please to show your papers, sir," and Webb took his passport from under the pillow and held the pencil flashlight so that the soldiers could read. The passport was taken roughly from him, muttered over by the thugs in uniform, stamped, and dropped on his berth. Then he blinked as a powerful light shone in his face and his bags were dragged down from the upper berth, opened, and their contents scattered carelessly on the berth, the floor, and the washbasin.

Finally the light snapped off, the three visitors went away, and the compartment door slid shut.

Webb cursed them softly. He was too tired to turn on the lights and repack Kaspar's clothes in Kaspar's bags. Instead he lay on his back, looking upward through the window at the full moon, listening to the beating of his heart, feeling the cold sponge of fear drip ice water along his spine.

There was no turning back any more. This was the moment you dreaded in the air—the point of no return—and for the first time he had passed it. Or had he passed it before, when he had made his compact with Nelda, when he had taken Loor's money? Had it been even earlier, when he had bummed his way from San Juan to San Francisco and began killing himself with nickel and dime smoke?

Looking at it one way, he was square with Loor. Because of Nelda, Loor had cared for him, given him back his health, cured him of wanting to drink, given him a challenge as well—a focal point of interest that had brought him through the thin days at Waverly. Well, Webb had kept his part of the bargain, even though he had counted on Ferdy to end the thing in Miami. So he was quits with Loor. The message had merely told him to wait for further instructions, and the fact of his absence would hardly cause them to speculate that he might have continued east. On the contrary; if a search were made for him, it would spread west and south from Zürich, certainly not toward Prague. The comrades had no idea he knew who the old man really was; even if they had, they would not reckon Webb as much of a danger. A Market Street stiff could be too easily discredited; no one would believe Webb if he were to shout that Jaro Capska had not died in the East River but had been intercepted and flown out of America to Europe. It was necessary to produce the body.

The phrase made his face contort in the darkness. You could not deny that there was every possibility that Capska had already confessed and had been killed, or had refused to reveal the names of his followers and had been tortured to death without mercy.

Webb knew that there was only one way to satisfy himself, to blot away the stain of his collaboration with Loor, and that was to bring back the old man—or find out if he had talked before he died. If he could do neither, Webb wondered if getting out of Czechoslovakia again would be worth the effort, and his head rolled slowly from side to side on the pillow in negation.

His eyes searched the horizon for the first light of dawn, but it was still too early. He had thought that he might lie awake until the train reached Prague so that he could scan the terrain for features he could remember in the future, but he realized that with his arrival in Prague he would need every gram of strength he could save.

He would be met, Frean had said. As Horton Palmer he would warrant official Czech notice; as Kaspar, even more. There was to be no difficulty about getting him into the heart of the Party, perhaps even an interview with Gottwald himself. The trick, Frean had said, the trick was to get out alive—with Jaro Capska.

Webb felt infantilely helpless. He was without even a pocket pistol, for Frean had warned him that carrying a weapon would cause unnecessary surveillance. He did not have so much as a penknife, although he intended to buy one in Prague, ostensibly as a souvenir. His baggage would be searched, he knew, and he was not to complain about it to anyone, or appear to notice that the STB had done its work clumsily. In the Party, you expected that, Frean had said. You spied on others, and were spied on in turn. He was not to take notes in public, or if he did, he should compose them as harmless notes on industrial efficiency that he could translate later when the need should arise.

When he had told Frean that his inability to speak Czech worried him, he had been told that too many chaps had depended upon language fluency in trying to pass as natives—that maybe two in a hundred could do it, and then only with immense luck. Webb had been told how frequently local allusions changed, and figures of speech altered with the times—things that could never be known in advance—so that by speaking only English, Webb would be far safer than if he knew the language and pretended to be a Czech. He was to remain as Kaspar until he was safely in Vienna or Trieste or Frankfurt, or wherever it was possible to take Capska. The old man was the important one, he told himself—not Jake Webb, the Caribbean bum. Whatever happened to Webb, the old man had to be freed, to be taken back to a country from which his voice could inspire the ones who had been left behind. For himself, Webb did not mind the hazard. He found it comparatively easy to face, for he had left nothing behind.

The station was filled with people, but none of them seemed to be going anywhere. They stood or sat or leaned against pillars, silent or talking in low tones. When men in uniform passed by, those who had been talking closed their lips and turned away.

As he stood in line, Webb noticed that the only men walking seemed to be making rounds, like night watchmen. They covered the station in pairs, stopping occasionally to demand papers from a woman or a youth, then standing immobile while the literate one of the two haltingly read the documents to the other.

Other stations Webb had known had been scenes of purposeful activity, of parting or arrival. Here, in Prague, the station seemed only to house a segment of the population that had nothing more pressing in their lives than waiting.

Waiting for what? Webb wondered. For a boxcar to take them to Siberia, or a flatcar to carry them to the uranium diggings at Karlovy Vary?

Probably not, Webb thought. When you went to forced-labor camp, you were taken from your bed at two in the morning, herded into a truck, and loaded aboard the boxcars in the railway yards. It was never done openly. Webb knew that the hopelessness in the peoples' eyes was there because they were prisoners in their own land, condemned to slavery in the scenes of their youth and old age.

A uniformed man behind a desk said something unintelligible and Webb took out his passport. He placed it on the desk in front of the man and said, "I speak only English."

The official said, "You are American?"

"Yes."

The man snorted. He opened the passport, saw the printed name, and blanched. He stood up quickly and said, "Excuse me, sir, for keeping you waiting." He stamped the passport quickly and handed it back to Webb. In a lower voice he said, "The committee has been waiting for you. They will take you to your hotel."

Webb stared at the man coldly. "Next time, do not keep me waiting." He walked away from the desk and saw a group of four well-dressed men come toward him. One of them held out his hand and said, "My dear Palmer, welcome to the People's Republic."

"Thank you," Webb said, accepting the man's hand briefly. "Your officials barricaded me for so long I wondered whether I should ever be received."

"Apologies," the man said. "Please forgive us, but we did not think it wise to tell too many of the special treatment we wished to accord you."

Webb smiled genially. "I understand," he said. "Say no more. I cannot let a minor annoyance blemish a day so long awaited."

"Quite so," the man said, and bowed gracefully. "Allow me to present myself, dear comrade. I am Rudolf Schier." He straightened and presented the others in turn: "Comrade Svermov of the

Coal Trust, Comrade Batovec of the Steel Trust, and Comrade Reise of the Foreign Office."

Webb shook hands formally with each official and said, "Gentlemen, I am indeed honored. I doubt that my small talents are worthy of so distinguished a reception."

Comrade Reise said, "It is not your talents, Comrade Palmer, so much as your services to the common cause that warrant your reception. Yet we were hesitant to arrange a large greeting, lest it attract hostile comment.

"You were quite right," Webb said. "And now may we leave the station? These staring people greatly disturb me."

"Surly dogs," Comrade Svermov said. "Unwilling to accept the inevitable, they must be forced like animals to accept the medicine of progress."

Rudolf Schier took Webb's arm at the elbow and steered him to a roped-off exit. "For Party members only," he said to Webb, and Webb said, "Like everything else."

Then they were inside a chauffeur-driven Tatra, the horn clearing a path down the crowded street, and as Webb turned to look at the façade of the station, he saw another car, smaller than the Tatra, pull away from the curb and follow fifty feet behind.

"Protection?" Webb asked, turning to Schier.

"Yes, comrade. A special guard of STB." He smiled proudly.

"Your organization?" Webb guessed.

Schier bowed his mead modestly. "Not so efficient as the omniscient MVD, but one must remember that we have only had the country since 1948."

Comrade Batovec ventured, "We felt alarm when you did not leave Zürich."

Webb held up his hand commandingly. "I held discussions concerning the Vistla Corporation," he said. "It was important that I discover the true reasons for their failure to the Party."

"Their *failure?*" Svermov almost shouted.

"Why, yes," Webb said coolly. "Can their inability to provide necessary equipment for Czechoslovakia be termed other than failure?"

Quickly Rudolf Schier said, "Of course not. The infiltration of spies and saboteurs within Vistla is well known. Their sabotage and deviationist activities have prevented the People's Republic from meeting it's mining quotas for the Soviet Union." He looked fixedly at Batovec. "It is the only possible explanation."

Webb turned to look at the streets, where red stars hung from buildings and store windows featured huge photographs of Stalin and Gottwald. Webb looked at the thick, peasant neck of the Communist dictator and felt his hands tighten involuntarily.

Everywhere there were placards with Communist symbols, cloth banners overhead with pictures of Comrade Stalin. The car felt suddenly stuffy, fetid, overcharged with repression. Webb rolled down a window and breathed deeply. He closed his eyes and said to the four Communists, "How good it is—how bracing to breathe fresh air," and the others murmured approvingly, but Webb knew that it would be a long time before he would feel anything faintly resembling freedom.

The Tatra turned smoothly into Stepanska and stopped in front of the Hotel Alcron. When the chauffeur opened the door, Webb saw another committee start out of the hotel to meet him. Holding his brief case, he stepped down from the car and smiled blandly through the Slovak greetings. Then he was in the hotel lift, his body tense until the door to his suite was opened, and when he was inside alone, when the bellboys and the manager had left, he lay back on the bed and tried to keep his body from shaking.

They gave a banquet to welcome him that noon. It was held in the auditorium of the Ministry of Industry on Na Frantisku, too far from Tesnov to let Webb catch a glimpse of the street as he was driven to the banquet in an official car.

The food was sickeningly rich. Course after course of lobster, sturgeon, suckling pig, whole lamb, white and red wines that Webb left untouched made him think of a harvest of overripe, bloated, but lovely toadstools, growing from the side of a fallen oak.

Rudolf Schier sat beside Webb during the banquet, translating the speeches, which repeated themselves in dreary and pedantic monotony. Webb found his eyes half closed as he listened to the eighth comrade, who was enunciating the doctrine of agricultural collectivization and quoting from Lenin. To Webb, it seemed that even a casual reader of the *Daily Worker* in New York could have parodied these speeches with their self-prostration to the idols of the October Revolution.

The collectivist enthusiast looked like a blacksmith dressed in his Sunday best, absurd behind the mounds of flowers, the white linen, the glint of well-polished silver, and the crystal glasses half filled with good wine. Webb leaned toward Schier and asked, "Who was this comrade before the coup?"

Schier smiled superiorly. "A tradesman, Comrade Palmer. One of the bourgeoisie."

"And now he's an agricultural expert?"

Schier nodded. "He possessed some small experience in repairing harrows and selling grain. However, he is an intellectually weak, vindictive opportunist who will be replaced as soon as Moscow finds a Russian able to handle the job."

"A necessity," Webb said. "The sooner, the better." He looked around the banquet tables, at the faces of the powerful men who had once been small, and the picture of Gulliver lying prostrate and bound by Lilliputians came into his mind and irritated him until he forced himself to listen to the restated phrases that Schier was repeating.

After a while the speeches ended and Schier said, "The chairman will call upon you to respond, Comrade Palmer, if you feel sufficiently rested from your long trip to address the comrades. I will be happy to translate your remarks for the others."

Webb said, "It will be better if no report is made of my having made a speech today," he said. "My position in America would be somewhat hazarded, were it made known by Trotskyite spies, and since I am en route to Moscow, I feel it would be better for me to hold my words until I have seen Comrade Stalin."

Schier nodded in agreement. "I quite understand." He raised a finger, and a waiter came to him, bowed, and listened while Schier gave him a message for the chairman. When the waiter had left, Schier said, "This concludes your official activities for the first day, Comrade Palmer. I have placed a car and an interpreter at your disposal for such use as you may wish to make of them. However, they are forbidden to take you beyond the city limits of Prague unless such a trip has been approved by myself."

"My stay will be so short," Webb said, "that I do not anticipate any reason to leave the city. Prague has so much to offer a visitor such as myself that I hope to become quite familiar with the city before I leave."

A brass band struck an opening chord, and the Comrades pushed back chairs and stood facing the pictures of Stalin and Gottwald. They sang in unison what Webb assumed to be the "Internationale." The words were meaningless to him, but he listened to the tune, so that he would recognize it when he heard it again.

The song had several stanzas, and the older men and women were growing red-faced from trying to outsing each other. Webb let his mind analyze the progress he had made so far. He was in Czechoslovakia, in Prague itself, and he had been accepted by the government and by the Party as an American Communist. So far, no one had said the name Kaspar to him, and he was glad that it had not yet been brought up. He needed time to familiarize himself with the Communist jargon, to gain confidence from the fact of his acceptance, before he could begin the plan his mind had been formulating.

Yet there was a problem connected with the length of his stay in Prague. He could not hope to stay more than a week at the most before questions would be asked regarding his reluctance to proceed to Moscow. And he supposed that he would have to accompany Party officials on inspection tours of Czech industry, for it was not likely that they would pass up an opportunity to have their country mentioned favorably in Moscow.

Webb knew that there were Russians in Prague—plenty of them. Horace Frean had given him a number that astounded him. So it was reasonable to suppose that among them would be agents of the MVD, who would not be slow to notice and report anything in Webb's conduct at variance with Palmer's background and planned itinerary. What it came down to was the simple conclusion he had known all along—the longer he stayed, the greater the danger became. Only five hours in Prague and he was nervous already—worried because he had not even learned if Capska were alive, or where he was being held. He had not bought the postcard photo of the Judas clock, or made an attempt to contact Herta Sebok at 73 Tesnov Street. Instead, he had been forced to talk with the reception committee, sit through a too rich banquet, and listen to speeches that spouted the most incredible trash he had ever heard.

The song of the Party ended, and during the applause Webb said, "I'm feeling a little tired, and I'd like to go back to my room."

"Surely," Schier said, and the two of them began moving toward the exit, as the crowd gave way respectfully before them. "Did you sleep badly last night?"

"Very badly. The train stopped quite often, and each time I was awakened."

"I am so sorry," Schier said. "The flight by air would have been more pleasant. The Russian authorities were seeking a man on your train. That is why it was stopped."

"Did they get the man?"

Schier shrugged. "They usually do." He stepped onto the sidewalk and opened the door of the car for Webb. "Your interpreter will wait in the hotel lobby for you, Comrade Palmer, and he will know how to get your car."

"Many thanks," Webb said, and they shook hands. The car moved away through Na Frantisku, and Webb thought, Maybe I can get a look at Tesnov Street on the way back. He leaned forward, touched the chauffeur's shoulder, and tried to speak to him in English, but the chauffeur's frightened reaction showed that he did not understand Webb's words and Webb sat back futilely until the car had reached the Alcron. This was a tough one, he thought. The contact that had sounded so easy in the room over the gift shop in Zürich was taking all his time to try to establish. The frustration was beginning to wear on him.

As he walked through the lobby, he saw a man get up from a chair and come toward him. The man took off his hat and bowed politely. He said, "I am your interpreter, sir, placed at your disposal by Comrade Schier."

Webb looked coldly at the man. "What's your name?"

"Laslo," the man said, fingering the brim of his hat. "You have only to—"

But Webb said rudely, "Please spare me the cataloguing of your services. I am perfectly aware of the privileges to which I am entitled, and when I desire any, you will be informed." He walked away from Laslo, toward the lift, without looking back.

Sitting at the writing table in his room, he tried to detect traces of its having been searched, but he could see nothing that was not as he had left it. Laslo, of course, would be from Schier's STB. Bellboys, charwomen, maids, and waiters would be plants or informers. His phone would be listened to, his room tapped with a microphone. He was sitting behind a two-way mirror, through which he could not see, but could be watched from the other side. He went to the window and looked at the profile of Hradcany Castle standing high on the hill beyond the Old Mill promontory with its spired, verdigrised roof, the long graceful arch of the Charles Bridge, and the quietly flowing water of the Vltava River. As he watched, a feeling of detachment came over him, as though he were secure in this room, so long as he stayed inside it, and within which time had no meaning. The sensation of departure from reality grew like a snake uncoiling, blunting his will to think and scheme and improvise; substituting instead a false sensation of security and immutability that he knew could destroy him as quickly as poison or the noose.

Forcing his thoughts back to the room, he walked to the door, listened to the quiet hallway, took off his shoes, and began to search the room for a microphone. He worked slowly, tapping the baseboards, then probing the cushioned furniture; next the lamps, the chandelier, and the wall pictures, making as little noise as possible, so that if his sounds were being recorded—and he was sure of it—the comrades would not know for certain whether he had failed or succeeded.

After half an hour he gave up and sat on the bed, wiping perspiration from his face, unknotting his tie. At least his search had sharpened his mind, focused it again on the problems that had to be solved. He took off his shirt and decided to have a shower. Over the telephone, he ordered a pitcher of ice water, and when he laid down the phone he looked down at the connection box under the table with its insulated wires leading in and out. He unscrewed the box with a nail file, working slowly and quietly, and saw something that made him breathe deeply and hold his breath. Two of the three wires from the phone cord were attached quite properly to terminals that connected with a wire leading along the baseboard and out of the room; the third wire was not connected with the other two, or to the terminals. Instead, it disappeared directly through a small hole that had been bored in the wall. Webb bent closely to look at it, and saw a few grains of plaster dust left carelessly behind by the drillers.

His room was tapped by the simple device of using the telephone diaphragm as a microphone. Webb got to his feet, stripped, and went into the shower. Finding the tap was the first tangible success he had experienced since leaving Zürich, and it acted like a shot of whisky. He opened the shower door and whistled the Communist song he had heard at the banquet.

CHAPTER EIGHT

THERE WAS a meeting that night at the home of Frantisek Krajcir, the Minister of Internal Trade, during which Webb listened gravely to the problems of the Communist Party in Czechoslovakia and commented only that the United States had not yet reached peak armament production, but that he had been given every reason to believe that America's World War III production would outstrip even the production of World War II, since the industrial tooling and reconversion problem was being met with the experience of 1940-45. His words caused some dissatisfaction, and one of the comrades ventured disbelief. Angrily Webb explained that equipment for infantry soldiers, for instance, was not likely to be modified greatly, and that once a factory received government orders, it had only to use the patterns, dies, and production techniques of the previous war to produce the necessary equipment.

Eventually the meeting ended, and Webb rode back to the center of town with Laslo. At Webb's request, the car drove through the Old Town Square and paused for a moment in front of the Town Hall. The Judas clock was lighted only by street lights and the hour was forty minutes away, so Webb suggested that he view the Ministry of Food, of which he had heard so much.

The car stopped in front of the darkened building, and while Laslo was explaining its architectural history, Webb looked at the other side of Tesnov Street for number 73. The number itself he found by locating numbers 71 and 75, then scanning the semidark space between long enough to see that 73 was a store that supplied stamp collectors. Webb smiled in the darkness, congratulating Horace Frean's friends on using so clever a point of contact—one that could normally receive correspondence from abroad, and to which it was only natural that foreign philatelists would apply when in Prague.

When Laslo had stopped speaking and turned to him, Webb said that he was tired and wanted to return to the Alcron. During the drive he watched carefully for landmarks, and was glad to see that the stamp store and the hotel were only a few blocks apart. In the lobby he bought a dozen photographic post cards, including one of the Judas clock, and while Lalso watched, paid a few koruny for the cards, placed them in his breast pocket, and walked toward the lift. Laslo started to follow him, but Webb said, "That's all for tonight, boy."

Laslo's face flushed. "Yes, sir. A factory inspection trip has been arranged for you tomorrow. We will leave here at ten-thirty."

"Can I get out of it?"

"Comrade Director Batovec of the Steel Trust would be very disappointed."

"Am I free for lunch?"

Laslo shook his head. "Luncheon will be at the tinplate factory."

"Speeches?"

"There are always speeches."

Webb said, "I shall be ready at ten-thirty." He stepped into the lift and got out at his floor.

Walking toward his room, he listened carefully, and before he opened the lock he put his ear to the door, but there were no alien sounds like the breathing of a man or the nervous shuffle of feet. He went into the room, turned on the light, locked the door, and looked into the bathroom and closets to make sure that he was alone. He took off his coat, loosened his tie, and wrapped a dressing robe around himself. Then he rang for the room attendant.

When the man came, Webb motioned him to close the door, and gave him a package of cigarettes. The man thanked him profusely, and Webb said, "Do you speak English?"

"Not so very good, sir, but I try understand what you say."

"Fine," Webb said. "Now tell me: How long do you work here each day?"

"From twelve to midnight, sir."

"Then you are free from midnight, tonight, until tomorrow at noon?"

"Yes, sir."

"Would you do a favor for me?"

The man bowed. "I would be honored, sir."

Webb turned toward the window so that the man could not see his face. He said, "In America I collect stamps—expensive ones. While I was in Zürich, I learned that a very rare one is soon to be brought to Prague. Without this stamp, my collection is meaningless, but with it, I shall be a very happy man." He turned and faced the attendant. "The last time I heard of the stamp, it was in a private collection in Belgrade, but the owner was liquidated by the heretic Tito, and the stamp was—shall I say prevented from falling into the hands of the Trotskyites. To be more brief, I learned that in order to purchase the stamp I must consult a woman named Herta Sebok at Seventy-three Tesnov. Have you heard of her?"

"No, sir."

"Remember the name well, and tomorrow morning go to Seventy-three Tesnov and inquire for Herta Sebok. Do you understand?"

"Yes, sir. And what shall I say regarding the business?"

"Only that a gentleman from America desires to talk with her regarding something of value now in Prague."

"And may I say that you are staying here?"

"By all means," Webb said. "My time is so occupied with official functions and Party matters that I fear I might leave Prague before obtaining what I want." He paused and looked meaningfully at the man. "Because I do not care to attract unnecessary attention to my dealings with Herta Sebok, it is more desirable that she visit me here."

The man bowed from the waist. "I understand, sir. Perfectly."

"But you must be discreet."

"Yes, sir."

"It would be unfortunate for you if the police were to learn of my transaction, for someone would have to be punished, and it would not, of course, be myself."

"I understand," the man said. "And when may you be visited by this Herta Sebok?"

"I leave it to you," Webb said. "You see me go and return each day. Arrange the time discreetly, and it will be greatly to your benefit."

"Your confidence is not misplaced," the man said, backing toward the door. He unlocked it, backed into the hall, and closed the door behind him. Webb went to the door, locked it again, and sat down on the bed. He looked at the double-purpose telephone, cradled so innocently on the desk, knowing that the attendant's report to the STB would be checked against their recorded conversation.

Perhaps the direct approach would prove to be the best one when the score was finally added back in Zürich. In any event, he had faced the fact that there was no way he could talk to Herta Sebok without others knowing that the contact had been made. By disguising the meeting as one motivated by personal greed and probable dishonesty, Webb felt that he had struck a note readily understandable to his STB surveillants. When Herta Sebok came, she would probably be smart enough to bring a stamp about which they could begin to talk. Then, as Webb declared it a forgery and insisted on examining it by the window or a light bulb, he could muffle the telephone with a towel and a pillow, and get down to the heart of the matter.

To Webb, taking off his shoes, it felt as though he had been pushing against a huge boulder for weeks, and had succeeded finally in destroying the balance of forces that had kept it motionless. In his mind, he could almost see the rock lurch forward and begin lumbering downhill into a valley filled with mist.

The next afternoon, after Webb returned from Comrade Director Batovec's new tin-plate mill, the attendant came to his room and announced that he had gone to 73 Tesnov in the morning and learned that Herta Sebok was not in Prague, but was expected within two days. The attendant had left Webb's message and nothing more. Webb gave him a handful of koruny and thanked him, feeling that he was not so far along as he had let himself hope. Now that he thought about it, it was possible that Herta Sebok would never come to him. She could have been caught by the STB or lost heart and left the resistance movement, or decided that the message from an American named Horton Palmer was so ambiguous as to point to an STB trap.

Tonight there was a meeting at which the problems of increasing uranium production in the Erz Gebirge would be discussed. Webb had noticed hostility among several of the officials when the agenda had been mentioned during the afternoon, and he realized with a feeling of warmth that in spite of the Vistla Corporation's past success in transshipping mining equipment, the inefficiency of the Russian engineers and the Czech forced laborers was taking an uncomfortable bite out of a production program whose goals themselves were absurdly high.

Webb had no particular interest in the mining program, for there was nothing he, as an individual, could do to sabotage it. Instead, he could only try to remember what he heard of names, tonnages, and equipment requirements, so that he could report them to Horace Frean when he next saw him.

Before the meeting there was a testimonial dinner to the Czech women's leader, Anezka Hodinova-Spurna, who looked like a conventional Midwesterner but spoke with the fanatic fervor of a revivalist. She was laying aside her work, it seemed, only long enough to visit Moscow, where she had been summoned to receive new instructions regarding the part that Communist women were to play in the stepped-up Communist campaign for world peace. The thought that he might be called upon to share a special flight to Moscow with Anezka Hodinova-Spurna gave Webb a cold feeling of urgency and frustration.

The night meeting with Schier, Batovec, Svermov, Reise, and others turned into a surprisingly profitless airing of complaints, charges, and countercharges. It was as though the Beaver Patrol had met to investigate the disappearance of eighty-seven cents from its treasury, with all the resultant small-boy recriminations and bitterness. So little had been accomplished that Webb did not even try to fix the occurrence in his mind. As the car crossed over the silent Vltava, returning to the Alcron, he noticed how few people walked at night.

He sat in his room, looking out of the window at the lights of Prague, hearing the rumble of traffic in Stepanska Street below, and feeling more alone than he had felt even at Waverly. It was the waiting that was bad. All of his life he had been impatient with the leisurely pace of people and events around him, and his impatience had kindled a conflagration that had burned him to a husk in the years since the war. There was a lesson to be learned from what had happened, and he knew now that there was nothing he could do but wait.

It was nearly midnight, a time in past years when he would have enjoyed a Scotch highball and a cigar if he were alone by himself in BOQ or a transient hotel room, but now even that simple pleasure was denied him. Other men, alone in hotel rooms in a strange city, would be writing letters to their wives and families or their friends or business associates, but Webb had none of those, and even if he had, his pose as Horton Palmer would prevent his writing to any but Palmer's intimates.

There was a bowl of fruit on the table, and as he went toward it to taste the grapes there was a knock at the door. He called, "Who is it?" and a woman's voice answered, "Fresh linen, sir."

Webb opened the door and saw a servant woman with apron, keys, and a stack of towels in her arms. She followed Webb into the room and closed the door behind her. Webb went back to the bowl of fruit and began eating the grapes. He could hear the woman in the bathroom, when suddenly she called to him, "What you want me to do with this, sir?"

"With what?"

"I have to show you."

"Just a minute, I'm coming." Webb walked into the bathroom and the woman closed the door. From under the apron appeared a small automatic pointed at Webb's chest. Her voice, different now, in clipped British words said, "You are a stamp enthusiast, Mr. Palmer?"

"Indeed I am."

"What kind of stamp had you in mind?"

"It's a rare one," he said. "Quite valuable. It has a picture of an old man on it. A Czech patriot."

"Masaryk?"

"No. A follower." He looked at the face of the woman, lighted brightly by the shaving bulb, and saw that she was not an old woman, but a young one. Her white face was thin, her high cheekbones accentuated by their lack of powder. She was small-boned and her tense face was expressionless. She said, "How did it get to Prague?"

"It was stolen," he said. "Stolen and flown here. But why would a mere linen maid be interested in rare stamps?"

"Because I am an enthusiast, myself, for things that are old and seldom seen nowadays."

"Then you know the stamp store at Seventy-three Tesnov?"

"Quite well." The gun did not waver. The girl's face was lean and intense as though she were playing tennis and anticipating a hard shot. "Have you seen much of Prague?"

"Almost enough," Webb said, "and I found one thing interesting beyond all else."

"What was that, Mr. Palmer?"

"Your clock," he said. "The one that Hanus built. I've never seen it strike the hour, but I have a picture of it that I look at frequently."

"I should like to see that picture."

"It's in my coat. I'll have to get it." Webb opened the bathroom door, went into the bedroom, took the clock postcard from his coat pocket, and threw the coat over the telephone. He went back to the bathroom, closed the door, and showed the picture to the girl.

Hardly looking at it, she said, "It is a very old clock."

"Perhaps too old," he said. "Would you know which is the Judas hour?"

The rubber-mask face began to relax. The lips said, "For each man, the hour is different."

Webb nodded slowly. "It matters not the hour, but the man."

And as he watched her, the pistol faltered; tears formed in her eyes, and he could see her teeth biting her lips to keep control of herself. Quickly he said, "It's over now, Herta. Each of us knows the other. It happened just the way he said it would."

"The man in Zürich?"

"Yes."

She walked forward, past him, putting the pistol out of sight under her apron, and into the bedroom. Webb followed, took a pillow from the bed, and molded it around the telephone. When he looked up she said, "So you found the microphone."

"The first day."

"There are no others," she said, sitting wearily on a chair. "These STB think they are too smart to be found out."

"They're only men," he said, and sat on the edge of the bed near her. As he looked at her face, he saw how tired she was—the little lines at the corners of her eyes, the exhausted slump of her shoulders—and he said, "You look half dead. When did you last sleep?"

"I hardly remember. When I got your message, I took a train and stood all the way to Prague."

"Where were you?"

"In Bratislava. I work there."

"As a linen maid?"

She smiled faintly. "No; not as a servant. As a scientist."

"A scientist?"

She nodded. "Once I taught physics at the Caroline University, but when the Party seized power, I was no longer allowed to teach. Instead, they gave me a job in a laboratory." She looked at Webb. "The walls of that laboratory are four feet thick and they are made of lead."

"I see," Webb said. "Something to do with atomic work."

"Something," the girl said. She looked around the room for a moment, then said, "You don't have a cigarette, do you?"

"Of course." Webb gave her one, lighted it, and left the pack lying on the bed.

"You don't smoke?"

"Not any more."

She inhaled deeply, gratefully. "They said you were a flyer. Is it because of that?"

"No."

"Are you a very good flyer?"

"I was," Webb said. "I can still get a plane off the ground and land it again."

"Can you fly European aircraft?"

"I flew a twin-engine Heinkel once. There's not too much difference. How far would I have to fly?"

"Perhaps very far," she said. "Switzerland or France."

"I could do it," Webb said. "Is that how we get him out?"

She nodded, and looked away from him. "It's how he came. I can think of no other way."

Webb took a deep breath. "How do we get the plane?"

"That is my responsibility."

"And the old man?"

"He is yours."

Webb got up from the bed, walked to the window, and said, "He's in town, you know. They've got him somewhere, trying to make him talk."

"I know." The cigarette trembled in her fingers.

"You know him?"

Wordlessly, she nodded.

"Is he worth all this?"

"Yes," she said suddenly. "He is worth both our lives."

Webb came back to the bed. "If you say so, I believe you. Now, tell me. What will we do?"

She stubbed out the cigarette. "He is an old man," she said. "Those who hold him will not think him capable of escape. Therefore, he will not be guarded heavily."

Webb nodded. "That makes sense."

"They will rely upon the power of their drugs, rather than upon bars and steel doors. But getting him to the plane is only half the problem."

"I can get him the rest of the way."

The girl-woman leaned forward. She said evenly, "Listen, American. There are fighter planes at Ruzyne waiting to shoot down stolen aircraft."

"We wouldn't do it by day," Webb said. "This is a night flight."

"Even so—"

"I dodged fighters for years," Webb said. "I flew the boxcars and the cattle crates—the big slow planes that carried men and equipment. You don't have to fly fast to keep alive; you just have to fly low."

She sat back, took another cigarette from the pack, and lighted it quickly. “I think you know your business,” she said. “I believe that you can do what you say.”

“Thanks,” Webb said dryly. “Now, how do we get to him?”

“Ask to see him,” Herta said. “Tell Schier you don’t think the STB is as efficient as the FBI. Let him brag. Then when he says the STB got Capska back from America, call him a liar until he shows Capska to you.” She shrugged and made a little gesture with her hand. “Once you have seen, you can return. By night.”

“Alone?”

“There will be others to help.”

“That’s better.”

“A car will be waiting. At Ruzyne a plane will have its engine turning over. A dash to the plane and he is safe.”

Webb smiled. “The way you tell it, it sounds like a midnight visit from Santa Claus.”

The girl did not smile. “I am serious, Mr.—Palmer. With you go the hopes of my country.”

“Are you a Czech?”

The girl nodded.

“But you speak English very well.”

“During the war I studied at the University of London.”

“And there you met Frean?”

“The man in Zürich?” She shook her head. “Not him. It was another. But to the same purpose.”

“And then you came back to Czechoslovakia.”

“I thought there would be peace.”

“So did we all,” Webb said, “but wasn’t it a nasty little trick they played on us?”

“It was horrible,” the girl said. “Horrible.” She turned away, and Webb could see her shoulders begin to shake. He held her arm firmly and said, “We’ve got a job to do, honey. Let’s not talk about it any more. The less we say, the better.”

Herta nodded and dried her eyes. She stubbed out the cigarette and asked, "Do you have a pistol?"

"Not yet."

She gave him hers. "I can get another, but for you it would be dangerous. They will not search you now. I read your speech in the paper tonight. They are glad you are here because they think you can tell them how to get more ore out of the Erz Gebirge."

"I'd be glad to blast it out for them, Webb said. "With a stick of bombs."

"You Americans think you can solve everything with your bombs."

"We can," Webb said. "The people with the bombs always have to correct the errors of the people who make the treaties."

"You do not care for the innocent people who will be killed?"

"No. Do you? I don't even much care what happens to your country. It was weak and it let a bunch of hoods take over. Now it's in trouble again."

"Your country could have prevented it."

"That's not my quarrel. Getting the old man back is a personal thing with me. I'd do it if he were a Rumanian or a Hungarian or a Jug."

"To salve your conscience?"

"Yes," Webb said evenly. "If you put it that way."

Herta Sebok rose from the chair. "Then we understand each other, American. We will do the thing, but for different reasons."

"That's right," Webb said.

"And if we succeed, what then?"

"There's a war going on," Webb said. "I'll try to get back in uniform."

"How brave," she said bitterly. "How brave one can become in a uniform."

"It takes a little guts," Webb said irritatedly. "A flyer's life isn't all officers' clubs and week ends in Paris."

"I'm sure it is not. But you might consider whether you could do more out of uniform."

Webb thought a moment. "I'm no good at this sort of thing," he said. "This is an accident. I'm only here by the coincidence of another man's death. So this job is comparatively easy."

"I'm glad you understand that."

Webb fought back his irritation. "I haven't enough languages. I couldn't pass for what I'm not, like the man in Zürich. He's a chameleon."

"At least you know your limitations," Herta Sebok said, and looked around the room. "Now, I must ask you for a place to sleep."

Webb indicated the other twin bed. "Help yourself."

"Thank you. I would not trouble you, but I am safer here than if I tried to go elsewhere. There is a curfew, you know."

"I know." He walked to one of the bureaus and said, "Here's an extra pair of pajamas, honey. They're Palmer's not mine, so you shouldn't mind wearing them."

"You're awfully antagonistic, aren't you?"

"I don't think so. Your country is your religion, but it doesn't happen to ring any bells with me. However, I'm tolerant. If different things motivate us, you might be a little tolerant, too." He looked at her sideways, and saw her turn from him, but not before he had seen tears on her cheeks. He took the clean handkerchief from his breast pocket, tossed it on the bed near her, and walked toward the door.

While he was opening the bolt, she asked, "Where are you going?"

"I'm not going to find another room, if that's what's on your mind. I'm going down to the lobby and act like a tourist."

"How?"

"I'm going to buy some books about historic Prague," he said. "One of them will have photographs and a floor plan of Hradcany Castle. You may know it like a poem, but I don't. I'm just a subaverage American who wishes he were fighting a nice clean war in North Africa again. In uniform." He opened the door, closed it behind him, and went down into the lobby.

When he had bought some more postcards, a Czech cigarette lighter, and the view book of Hradcany Castle, he saw a man sitting in the chair where Laslo usually sat, nodded toward him, and went back to the room.

The lights were out when he opened the door, but he could hear her breathing from the bed.

For a long time before he went to sleep, he lay awake in the moonlit room, aware of her presence only a few feet away, knowing that she was lying awake. Then, finally, he heard her breathing soften into a subdued rhythm, and he let himself fall asleep, too.

CHAPTER NINE

IN THE REAR of the stamp store at 73 Tesnov, he sat facing three men whom Herta had brought him to meet. Behind him stood an old woman they called Marika, serving the men midmorning *pareks* and beer. Beside him sat Herta, eating a *parek*, and when Webb tried one, he found it was only a well-spiced frankfurter. Instead of Pilsen beer, he drank milk that Marika grudgingly supplied, and watched the faces of the three men who were to aid him in freeing Jaro Capska.

Karlo, Eduard, and Czarny ate greedily and drank their beer as though they were on safari. To Webb, it seemed unreal that, with luck, tomorrow night the four of them would be at Hradcany Castle, risking their lives for the sake of an old man.

Eduard was to drive the car and wait outside the castle pretending to adjust the carburetor while Karlo, Czarny, and Webb were inside. Another man was to be at the airport, checking the engines of a converted German bomber; the tanks would be filled, and there would be charts and parachutes.

Even being at 73 Tesnov seemed unreal. Webb had avoided Laslo by saying that he had a stomach upset and planned to spend the morning in bed, then leaving by the rear stairs and the alley exit. If his absence were discovered, a serach would certainly be made. But it was a chance they had to take. Later in the day, he was to see Schier and tell him some things he had learned about FBI operations in America.

The men finished their *pareks* and beer, looked hopefully at the glowering Marika, and finally at Herta, who was to do the interpreting. She began to speak to them, slowly at first, then more rapidly, looking at Webb and gesturing slightly as she spoke. When she had finished, she spread a ground plan of the castle on the floor and spoke to Webb. "There was a time when this place was open to everyone. We came on Sunday afternoons and played hide-and-seek behind the big chairs." She gestured toward the three men. "They know it well," she said. "Every meter of it."

"Thank God for that," Webb said.

Her finger traced a route on the map. It was the road to the castle, the path to the entrance. "There will be no guards until you reach the castle," she said. "The sergeant of the guard makes his rounds so that he passes each post every nineteen minutes."

"How do we get past the guards?"

"You kill them," she said without emotion.

"What about the noise?"

Herta said something, and Karlo drew an air pistol from his trousers pocket. He handed it to Webb.

Herta said, "This is a rather special weapon. In the first place, it holds fifteen shots, in the second, it is powerful enough to penetrate a man's chest and kill him."

"I haven't seen many air pistols. I thought they had to be pumped by hand to get firing pressure."

Herta shook her head. "The British improved on that. The grip of this pistol is simply a shaped flask of carbon dioxide under very great pressure. When fifteen shots have been fired, the pressure is dissipated and the flash must be charged again."

Webb felt the balance of the pistol and said, "I'd rather have something that makes a little noise. Like a Colt forty-five."

Herta took back the pistol and gave it to Karlo again. "A conventional gun is fine for your uniform war, Amercan; but here we must use more subtle methods." She looked at Webb. "Now you understand about the guards."

"I understand."

She paused, and spoke to the men, then to Webb. "The castle is not well lighted at night." She smiled a little. "Perhaps President Gottwald is afraid of an air raid." Her finger crossed over the castle wall and followed a passageway to the right. "Information has come to us this morning that Jaro Capska is probably in this room. It is on the ground level. You can find out when you go there."

"With Schier?"

Herta nodded, and her blonde hair fell momentarily across her face. She brushed it back, and Webb noticed the high cheekbones and the small tilted nose. There was only a trace of lipstick on her lips, and the muscles of her face moved smoothly as she talked. To Webb, she looked entirely different than in her disguise of last night. This morning she looked like a girl you'd like to have your sister bring over to play tennis with.

He listened as she spoke, briefing them on the plan, making sure each man knew his part and the over-all time schedule. Then, when she had finished, there were no further questions, and Webb realized that he had heard everything that was to be said on the subject. There was nothing else. All of them were silent for a moment until Herta rolled up the map and gave it to Marika, who took it to the front of the shop. Then they got up from their chairs and began to leave at intervals. When only Herta and Webb were left, he said, "I've heard full colonels do worse briefing than that, honey. I think you know what you're doing."

"I have to," she said simply. "All of us have to know. If we didn't, we couldn't survive."

Webb lighted her cigarette and asked, "What will you do after tomorrow night, Herta?"

She shrugged and looked away. "Go back to Bratislava. Wait for the next job that has to be done."

"And that's your life," Webb said.

"That's what it has become."

"I've never asked you if you're married."

She shook her head slowly. "I am not married. My young man was taken prisoner by the Russians for forced labor."

"Couldn't he be alive somewhere?"

"It is nice of you to think that, but he was taken three years ago. In Russian lumber camps there are a few prisoners who survive the first winter; many less the second." She exhaled slowly and looked toward the wall. "There are no three-winter prisoners."

"I'm sorry," Webb said. "I should have realized you had your own reasons, too." He walked to the door and said, "I'm lunching with Schier, you know. When will I see you again?"

"Tonight. I'll come the same way."

Webb smiled. "I'll save a bed for you," he said.

He walked from Tesnov Street down to the National Theatre on Narodni Trida, by the quay, then to Wenceslas Square, and finally into the Old Town Square. The time was five minutes of eleven, and Webb leaned against a wall, pretending to read a newspaper, until the Hanus clock began to strike. He watched, fascinated by the sepulchrally grotesque motions of the carved figures—the skeleton, Judas, the group from the Last Supper, and the crowing cock. Everything happened as Horace Frean had described it. Then the cock was silent, the clock was inanimate again, and Webb folded the newspaper under his arm and began walking back to the Alcron.

Director Schier was driving him to a luncheon at Libeznice for a group of superquota miners, when Webb spoke to him about the STB. He said, "If you treat every visitor as crudely as I have been handled, Comrade Schier, I believe you are making a mistake."

"Have you not been treated to your satisfaction? Is there any way in which we have failed you?"

"One," Webb said, looking at Schier. "If you have meant to disguise the fact that I have been under surveillance, you failed miserably."

Schier looked away from him. “I had no choice,” he said. “It is so in every case—even for one as well regarded as yourself.” He looked back at Webb. “The order came from Comrade Gottwald himself.” His voice grew lower, so that the chauffeur would not hear. “It is understood that he is acting in accordance with the wishes of Comrade Stalin.”

Webb shook his head. “My dear comrade, I do not question the advisability of keeping close watch on visitors from abroad. That is very wise, of course. But you are clumsy,” he said. “At the risk of sounding disloyal, I must tell you that the American FBI handles such matters in a far more subtle way.”

“The FBI!” Schier said angrily. “Fascist jailers!” He lowered his voice again, and asked Webb, “You know something of their methods?”

“I have made it my concern to learn what I could of our enemies.”

“You will tell these things to me?”

“Of course,” Webb said. “For instance, a comrade seldom knows that he is under FBI surveillance. So he discards caution and moves freely, making contacts he should have kept hidden. If he were to know he were being watched, the contact might never be made, and some other method would have to be used.”

“Very clever,” Schier agreed reluctantly. “What else?”

“The FBI would not bother to run an extra wire into a comrade’s telephone. Instead, they would use ventilators, light sockets, and the comrade’s radio.”

“The radio?”

“Naturally. By installing a small part, the receiving set becomes a transmitter, sending to a nearby place all conversation within its range.”

“Marvelous,” Schier said. “Yet Eisler escaped.”

“True,” Webb said. “Although I have heard it said he was permitted to leave as an alternative to lengthy prosecution, and in the hope that he would reveal his contacts during the ocean crossing."

"But the *Batory*, on which he escaped, is a Polish ship!"

Webb nodded. "A ship riddled with spies and informers of the FBI."

Schier's face paled. "Of this you are certain?"

Webb's face hardened. "Do you doubt me?"

"No, no," Schier said hastily. "No, Comrade Palmer. Of course not. But the intelligence is so incredible..."

Smoothly Webb said, "And therefore valuable to Director Schier of the STB."

Schier nodded thoughtfully. "And you will tell no one else?"

"Why should I?" Webb asked cheerfully. "Comrade Schier is the appropriate official to whom such intelligence is to be entrusted. You may count on my discretion."

"Your generosity is not unappreciated, Comrade Palmer. Believe me, if my beetles have been less than subtle in comparison to the FBI, there is also a score on which the FBI failed badly—to the high credit of the STB."

"In what way?" Webb asked skeptically.

Schier's voice became appropriately confidential. "You remember that the People's Republic of Czechoslovakia was once represented at the United Nations by a man called Jaro Capska?"

"I remember the name." Webb paused. "In fact, we were introduced on Long Island shortly before he committed suicide."

Schier smiled. "Good. Then you would recognize this same Jaro Capska?"

Webb nodded. "Unless the worms have eaten away his face."

Schier leaned closer, and almost in a whisper said, "Capska is not dead."

"Not dead? He drowned in his automobile. The body was later regained and buried. High Washington officials attended his funeral."

Schier shook his head in a superior manner. "Not Capska's," he said. "The cortege did honor only to the corpse of a pauper."

"And the STB was responsible?"

Schier nodded proudly. "No other. Through our contacts in America, the traitor Capska was intercepted and flown back to Europe incognito."

"Incredible," Webb said. "And this same Capska is now in your hands, alive?"

Schier shrugged. "Less alive than dead," he said. "Our methods have not served to improve his health."

Webb felt his spine grow cold. He wanted to jam the nose of his pistol into Schier's belly, pull the trigger twice, then watch him squirm and beg for death. Controlling himself, he said, "And this clever thing has actually been accomplished?"

"You will see for yourself," Schier gloated. "You will see an enemy of the people still struggling to preserve his antirevolutionary confidences." His face saddened. "And I am afraid that death will permit him to succeed."

"A tragedy," Webb agreed. "The drugs are too powerful?"

"For so old a man as he. They rob the body of its will to resist; even of its will to live. At his age he can scarcely survive another week of questioning."

Webb looked out of the window, at the fields and pleasant trees of Libeznice, so that Schier could not see his face. "He has told you nothing?"

Schier cursed. "Lies. Only lies that are quickly found out. The doctor cannot understand how his mind is still able to resist our questions."

Webb waited a moment, took a deep breath, then spoke in a casual voice. "I should like to see this Lazarus from the tomb," he said. "Unless you are unable to arrange it."

Loudly Schier said, "There is nothing I cannot arrange, Comrade Palmer. We will go to the castle as soon as we have had luncheon." He paused and looked at Webb. "I suppose these dirty laborers bore you as much as they do me?"

"Infinitely," Webb said. "They are little better than animals, and flattering them to produce our goals is not the way I would have it."

"Nor I," Schier said. "To flatter them is time-consuming, besides being boring. The lash consumes little time and produces predictable results."

Webb smiled. "Efficiency," he said. "I recommend your method if only for its efficiency."

When he came back from the castle, back to the security of his room after seeing what Schier had shown him, his mind was numb with rage and his body felt like stone. He paced the floor of his room, craving something to quiet his nerves; something that would make him forget the ashen face of the half-mad old man who babbled idiotically when Schier spoke to him. Webb's own guilt clawed at his mind like an eagle's talons, and suddenly he found it unbearable. Calling the bar, he ordered a bottle of whisky and some ice, then opened his collar and waited, his throat wet with perspiration, his hands opening and closing, until the bellboy came.

Webb mixed the drink carefully, one-fourth Scotch, three-fourths water, then went to a chair beside the window and began to drink. The whisky tasted musty and disagreeable, like the memory of childhood medicine, and he fought to make his stomach accept it. But before the liquor was able to bring him even the first glow of well-feeling, Webb felt his stomach turn over, and he walked rapidly to the bathroom.

Weak from retching, nauseated almost beyond endurance, he stripped off his clothes and turned on the shower. Still shivering under the hot water, he massaged his chest and neck and legs in an effort to restore his chilled circulation; to relax the tense nerves of his throat and stomach. Then, finally, when the bathroom was thick with steam, he felt warmth come again to his body, and the spasmodic contractions of his stomach eased and then stopped.

He dried himself, put on pajamas and a dressing robe, and ordered a glass of hot milk. When he finished it, he took the pistol Herta had given him, felt its potent weight on his hand, and slipped it into a pocket of the dressing robe. He had decided to put on some clothes when the telephone rang. Its insistent clangor startled him, and he let it ring four times before he picked it up.

"This is Director Schier," the voice said. "I have some agreeable news for you."

"Excellent," Webb said, feeling his throat grow dry. "What is it?"

"You will leave for your destination tomorrow. It is all arranged."

"Excellent," Webb said again. "Am I to thank you for the rapidity of my departure?"

"Not alone myself," Schier said. "We have been awaiting the arrival of a third comrade to join you and Comrade Hodinova-Spurna on the long flight."

"What is the departure time?"

"Ten in the morning," Schier said. "Will you be prepared?"

"I'll be ready," Webb said, and hung up, shocked by the change in schedule.

Unless he were to become a fugitive in Prague, he would have to fly Capska out of Czechoslovakia tonight. That meant he must find Herta and advance their plan by twenty-four hours. The arrival of the other comrade was one of the incalculables around which he must devise an alternative route. So far, until the phone call, he had been luckier than he had had any reason to expect, but now the pendulum was beginning to swing the other way. It would be a race against time and events, with the odds against him increasing as the hours were tolled off on the Judas clock.

Almost unconsciously his mind began to review and check the time schedule for Capska, the way it had been trained to do before a take-off. He looked at the almost full bottle of whisky, grimaced, and walked toward the bathroom for his clothes.

A knock at the door halted him, and he called "Who is it?" thinking that if it were a bellboy, he would tell him to come back later, but the voice answered, "Fresh linen, sir," and he knew that it was Herta.

He bolted the door behind her, muffled the telephone, and in a rush of words told her what Schier had said. Calmly she placed her pile of towels on a chair and said, "Are you afraid to go through with it now?"

"No."

She said, "But then, you haven't really much choice, have you? Either you fly west tonight, or a plane takes you to Moscow tomorrow, where you will certainly be killed."

Webb caught her by the wrists and said, "Things are on a different basis now. I taunted Schier the way you suggested, and he showed me the place they keep Capska."

Her features became very still. "You saw Jaro Capska?"

Webb nodded. "I saw him—or what's left of him—and the way I feel about getting him out of there is different now. Even if we're killed or the plane crashes before we're free, it'll be worth the try just to get him away from those devils." He dropped her wrists and walked toward the window. "Capska's more than just an old man," he said. "If exchanging places with him would do any good, I'd do it tonight. But someone has to fly the plane, and since I got him here, I'll get him out."

"And your own conscience?" Her words were curiously soft.

"This isn't just for me any more. It's for Capska and what he stands for, and for you and Karlo and Czarny, and against the torturing devils like Schier and Fierlinger and Gottwald. It's a simple issue, Herta. I should have found it before."

"But you've found it when it counts," she said, and put her arms around his shoulders from behind. "I'll miss you more than you'll ever know."

Webb turned and drew her to him. "You're coming with me," he said. "Tonight."

"I can't."

"I'll force you to come, Herta."

"No. I have to stay here. There are too many people who depend on me."

"To hell with them. There are only three people in our world now. You and I and the old man I once betrayed. Karlo and Eduard and Czarny are staying behind. They're men. Let them do the job you've been doing."

"I've done a man's job," she said. "I couldn't stop now, no matter how much I might want to leave with you."

"Then I'll stay here," he said. "You can't make me leave."

She touched his forehead and smiled. "I'd have to hide you," she said. "Feed you and be your eyes and ears. If I did that, I wouldn't have much time for anything else. Not that I wouldn't like to be that for you."

"Or that I wouldn't like to have you," he said, and kissed her very gently. Her lips softened and met his with a firmness and a seeking passion that he would not have believed had he not now felt it. Then he said to her, "I'd like you to know my name, sweetheart."

"Yes. Please tell me."

"Jake," he said. "Jake Webb."

"I love you, Jake," she said, "and if it were possible to have a home and children, I'd want them with you."

"We'll have all of that," he said. "I can't see it in the cards yet, but it must be there, somewhere ahead of us, next week or next month or next year." He fumbled with her maid's apron, her plain gray blouse, and the knot that drew her blonde hair back from her face. Then he turned off the light in the room and his dressing robe slid to the floor.

Her lips were on his then, and her passion was strong enough to make her sob as he took her, and later, when their bodies were their own again, he could still feel the fusing of minds that had been theirs from the moment they were one.

Only half awake, he felt her go from him; heard her dressing, then the little tinkle of her keys. She came back to the bed without turning on the light and said, "I must go now to tell the others. There is only a little time."

"But you'll be back tonight?"

"I hope so. But I cannot go with you to the castle. If we see each other again, it will be at the plane."

He drew her to him in a spasm of fear, and said hoarsely, "And after tonight? Where will you be then?"

"In Bratislava, I hope."

"How would I find you there?"

He could feel her heart pounding before she answered him. "There is a little shop on Michalska Street, called Domace. It is exactly to the left of St. Michael's gate. Someone is always there, even when the shop is closed. If someone were to ask for Herta Sebok, it would be told to me."

He kissed her and let her go with leaden reluctance. In the darkness he heard her whisper, "God bless you, my Jake," and then the door opened and closed, and she was gone.

Webb turned over, and felt the catching of his breath enlarge into a spasmodic shaking of his body. Tears did not come to his eyes, but his throat tightened unbearably, and he knew that he was utterly drained emotionally. The weakness of loneliness seemed to paralyze him, but he fought it off, finally, forced himself into a cold shower, and put on a business suit with the pistol in his hip pocket. His watch told him that he had nearly two hours before the meeting with the car, and he decided that he would try to eat something.

In his room he ate a greasy meal of dumplings, roast goose, and coffee, and when he was taking Palmer's passport from the brief case, the telephone rang. Thinking it might be Herta or Karlo, he answered it, but turned cold when he heard Schier's voice. "The other comrade is in the hotel, and would like the pleasure of a drink with you."

"Some other time," Webb said. "I'm busy packing and my stomach feels lousy."

"But this comrade is very important to the Party," Schier persisted. "She has been summoned to Moscow to receive orders for the American continents, as comrade Hodinova-Spurna will receive orders for Central Europe."

A woman, Webb thought. He had not known that before. If he refused to see her, Schier might become suspicious. If he saw her, perhaps he could learn something worth while for Horace Frean. He said, "I'll be glad to see her. Will you be with her?"

"No," Schier said. "I am not so privileged. But I believe she has a message for you."

"Very good."

"Her room is only three doors from yours, on the left. She asked that you come directly, without calling."

"I'm on my way," Webb said, "but I can't stay long. I'm sure she has packing to do, too." He hung up, adjusted his tie, combed his hair, and went into the hallway.

When he knocked at the door, a voice said, "Come in, please," and inside, he saw a woman standing with her back to him talking on the telephone. He went into the sitting room, where a tray of liquor bottles and ice had been placed on a table, and began to open a bottle of Karlovy Vary for himself. While he poured the bubbling water into a glass, the woman put down the telephone and turned to him. He felt himself chill.

The woman was Nelda.

Her face stiffened, she started to say something, then turned quickly and reached for the telephone. In an instant Webb's muscles thawed and he was at her side before she could speak into the receiver. With one hand he ripped out the telephone cord and tried to hold her, but she fled from him, around the chaise longue toward her purse, and fumbled at it to pull out the small gun inside. Webb picked up a bottle of liquor and threw it.

The bottle caught her near the throat, knocking her backward against a chair, and the gun dropped to the floor. A gurgling scream caught in her throat as his hands went around it. Her fingernails raked at his face, her legs and knees kicked at his groin and his belly, but he half turned from her so that the crippling blows glanced harmlessly off his hip and his thigh. Then her hands and nails were clawing at his wrists, stripping flesh from them until he saw his own blood begin to flow, but in spite of the pain he knew that he must choke her until she could struggle no more.

As he watched, a look of incredulity came over her face, swollen red with trapped blood, and it seemed to change color. Her struggles stopped gradually, and then her hands dropped limply to her sides. Webb dug his thumbs into her larynx and felt a strange animal exultation come over him. Her hips twitched once, and then her legs straightened spasmodically, and she was dead. Webb gasped for air, for he had been holding his own breath while he choked her. His bloody hands came slowly away from her throat, their fingers still curved in a kind of rigor, and when he looked at the dead, lusterless eyes, he began to sob. Slowly he put his head to her breast to hear any heartbeats, but there were none he could detect. The struggle had torn her dress so that one breast was almost exposed and her hair had become uncoiled. One braid lay across her white shoulder like a black serpent, and as he looked at the woman he had killed, an obscene spasm flowed through his body, sickening him with its strength, until he turned away and stumbled toward the bathroom.

As the cold water stung the lacerations on his wrists, he realized that he and Nelda had not even exchanged a word. In their brief moment of recognition, each had known what he must do, and like panther and deer, they had begun the chase of death. To have shot her would have aroused the hotel. To do anything, in fact, but what he had done would have been suicidally foolish. When Nelda went for her gun, he knew that she meant to kill him, and by all the laws of nature and war, he had been justified in strangling her.

A fantastic montage of memories swept through his mind as he bathed his face—Nelda swimming with him; Nelda beside his bed at Waverly; in the woods with him that afternoon; in the hotel at Miami Beach.

And now she was dead. A corpse lay in the next room staring at the ceiling, growing cold. The corpse of a woman he had wanted once, and with whom he had once mated as passionately as though the two of them were animals in rut.

He dried his face and hands, crossed the sitting room without looking at the strangely contorted body, and went into the bedroom. On her dressing table was a bottle of astringent lotion he had seen before, and he poured it on his wounds. The alcohol burned like a dozen branding irons, but he put some of it on his face as well, for it felt puffy and strained.

He knew that he must leave her now. Perhaps an electrician was already outside the door, ready to repair the break in the telephone connection. Because only Schier would know that he had been the last to see her, the hunt would not immediately turn to him. But in any event he must leave the hotel and find his way toward the rendezvous at the Judas clock.

In the sitting room, he looked once more at the obscenely postured body with its staring, focusless eyes, then turned off all the lights. He put his ear to the door, and when he could hear nothing in the corridor, went out quickly. In his own room the phone was ringing in its far-off, muffled way, but he did not answer it. Instead, he opened Kaspar's brief case and took out the maps and plans he would need before the night was over. He felt the passport in his pocket, folded the other papers into his coat, and turned off the lights. The blood on his hands and wrists had congealed, making them stiff and painful, and it hurt him to open the door.

There was a porter in the hallway, knocking at Nelda's room, but he did not see Webb pass the elevator and go down the back stairs.

In the alley Webb walked close to the building until he was on the small back street behind the Alcron; then he stepped out boldly toward Malostranske Namesti Square, where the crowd would be thickest. He had an hour and a half to wait before going to the Old Town Square.

He paused to buy a hat from a shop that was still open, then moved on. The shriek of a policeman's whistle halted him for an instant, but he regained his stride and looked slowly around. It was only a traffic policeman signaling at an intersection, but Webb felt a band of ice around his neck. His throat dry, his breathing quick and irregular, Webb moved from under a street light and merged with the crowd ahead.

CHAPTER TEN

He sat in the corner of a café less than a block from the Judas clock. A cup of coffee was in front of him, next to a small glass of plum brandy, which he did not intend to drink. He was pretending to read a newspaper, and his eyes had grown tired from following columns of unfamiliar words, and he knew he could not keep it up much longer. The time was too soon to start walking toward the rendezvous, and a man sitting in a café attracted less attention than one walking aimlessly along a darkened street. The rescuers had to be at the castle by curfew time, after which there would be only a few cars on the road to Ruzyne, and those official.

Somewhere in Prague the girl he loved would be talking with three men, keeping up their spirits, watching the time, and thinking about the American who was to fly an old man out of Prague that night. Webb was glad she did not yet know that he had killed Nelda, but when the police found out, Herta would hear and wonder why he had done it so brutally.

A loud-speaker truck turned the corner, blaring what Webb believed to be a political exhortation, for the sides of the truck carried hammer-and-sickle insignia. Few of the café patrons looked up from their coffee and brandy, nor did the waiters seem to pay any attention to the truck's loud message. He looked carefully at his watch and saw that only fifteen minutes remained. By now, Nelda's body would have been discovered and Rudolf Schier notified. Because Schier had never learned that the man who posed as Horton Palmer was a flyer, Webb's chances of getting to the airport and into a plane were better than he had first believed. But although before Nelda's death the police had not been looking for him, they undoubtedly were at this moment, and the thought made him stare more fixedly at his newspaper.

Two men in trench coats and narrow-brimmed hats came around the corner, stood by the café entrance, and looked at the customers. Webb forced his hand to reach for the cup of cold coffee and bring it to his lips. When his hand lowered the cup to the tabletop, he moved the newspaper slightly, as though continuing a column elsewhere on the page. The move shielded his face from the line of sight to the entrance, and when he finally looked again, the trench-coated men had moved on.

He hoped that the three men he was about to meet would bring heavier weapons than the air pistols they had shown him, for if they encountered road blocks, they would have to shoot their way through, even at the risk of Capska's being wounded or killed. Webb knew how to handle a tommy gun; he had kept one in the cabin of his transport, swinging from the ceiling within reach in case of a forced landing behind the lines. But the hope that Eduard, Karlo, and Czarny had an automatic weapon was small, and even if they had anything in that line, it would probably be a Schmeisser machine pistol or a Russian burp gun, neither of which Webb knew how to fire. He looked at his striated hands where new brown scabs were forming to replace the strips of skin gouged out by Nelda's nails. His wrists were as raw as though torn by a mad dog, and as he closed his eyes he could see the frantic look of her face, feel the desperate, frenetic efforts of her hands and fingers. He knew that now he was a murderer, yet he felt no sense of guilt beyond what he had known during the war, for she had been an enemy as surely as those men in uniform.

Five minutes more, his watch told him, and his skin began to prickle with anticipation. A waiter took away his coffee, and Webb took the brandy glass between his fingers, twirled it, and raised it to his lips, but he did not drink. Even the fumes made his stomach react a little, and he put the brandy down and looked at the street. The café was behind the Town Hall, so he would not have to cross the open square alone to rendezvous with the car. So far, he did not even know what kind of car they were using. It would be one that had been stolen earlier in the evening, preventing a trail to the three Czechs who were going with him tonight.

Three minutes left. He licked his lips, pulled some koruny and heller from his pocket, and laid them on the table. Then he folded the newspaper over his arm so that no one could see him take the pistol in his hand and hold it under the fold of the paper. He got up from the table slowly and walked to the doorway. As he reached it, he heard hurried footsteps behind him, and turned, fully expecting to have to shoot the man, but it was only the waiter saying something in Slovak and handing him back two of the bills he had left. Webb nodded politely, stuffed the bills in his pocket with his left hand, and holding the disguised pistol in his right, went out to the sidewalk and turned toward the Town Hall.

As he forced himself into a measured pace, he realized briefly that now was the moment of take-off when there could be no turning back without death. He counted each step to steady his mind, and then he was at the corner of the square with the Judas clock only fifty feet away.

One minute to go by his watch, but already the old clock of Hanus had begun to mark the hour, and as he listened to the ancient machinery grind the carved figures into action, a small sedan turned into the square from the street down which he had been walking. The sedan slowed in the square, and when he was under the clock, hearing the figure of Judas shake its moneybags, a small light shone briefly through the window. Webb stepped to the curb, the car door opened, and he got inside.

Eduard was driving. Webb sat on the rear seat between Karlo and Czarny. The three Czechs wore army uniforms of the People's Republic, and an automatic weapon lay across Karlo's knees.

Karlo said, "I hear you kill someone?"

Webb nodded.

"You know her?"

"Yes."

"Too bad we do this tonight. Tomorrow better, because I know one guard then."

"Aren't we going to kill the guards?"

Karlo nodded. "This one I know, I want to kill."

Czarny had said nothing. Webb saw him watching the intersections as the car moved up the long hill toward Hradcany Castle, and looking at a radium-dial wrist watch. Beside him, Karlo shifted the automatic weapon between his knees and said something to Czarny, who grunted in answer.

As the car turned again, Webb could see the lights of Prague below, the moonlight shining on the Vltava, the long arched outline of the Charles Bridge. To Karlo he said, "If we get Capska out, where do I land the plane?"

"Linz," Karlo said. "You are expected there."

"How far is it?"

"Not far in a plane. One hundred thirty miles."

"Which direction?"

"South," Karlo said. He took a folded paper from his blouse and gave it to Webb. "All marked," he said. "Easy to find.

"Who runs the airport? Russians?"

Karlo shook his head. "English. British Zone of Austria."

"How far is Vienna?"

"Don't know. Not far."

"Bratislava?"

"Near Vienna."

Webb took the charts, put them inside his coat pocket, and threw the newspaper out of the car window. He held the pistol in his right hand, pulled back the receiver slide, and let it push a shell in the chamber. Karlo pushed aside the pistol and said, "Not yet, American. Inside Hradcany we use the air pistols."

Webb nodded and put away the automatic, feeling vacantly helpless without a weapon for the job that had yet to be done. The car began to slow, and when Webb looked out he could see that Eduard was turning them toward the small south entrance to the castle, where there were only two guards, where the access to Capska's cell was more direct. Karlo touched his arm with the nose of an air pistol and said, "You walk between us like prisoner," and Webb nodded again.

When the car stopped, Eduard opened the door toward the castle entrance and Czarny studied his watch. Webb, looking toward the guard posts beside the entrance, saw the guard sergeant leave the entrance post and walk to the west, then turn around a bastion and disappear. Czarny said something sharply and stepped out of the car. He walked directly toward the guard posts while Webb and Karlo piled out behind him and began walking up the incline. Webb could feel his heart pound urgently and an almost forgotten sense of elation flowed through his body, strengthening his stride and making him gulp the cool night air.

Walking between them now, he pulled his hat down over his forehead and saw the two guards standing on either side of a lighted area. The three men were almost upon them when a guard shouted something and Czarny slowed and answered him in an irritable voice. The other guard pointed a rifle at the party, but the three kept coming until all five men stood almost in a row under the light, and while Czarny was talking to his guard, facing him under the light, he shot him twice, once in the throat, then in the head, as the guard stumbled forward, clawing at his killer. The rifle almost clattered to the concrete, but Webb caught it and propped it inside the guard post. When he looked around again he saw the other guard crumpling to the ground and Karlo returning his gun to his pocket. The two bodies were pushed back out of sight, and before Webb moved into the castle, he saw one body slump slackly into a corner. The noise of the three shots had been less than a muffled cough, and Webb realized how right they were to use silent weapons for a job like this.

They were dependent upon him now, and Webb saw quickly where the main corridor from the front entrance joined the gallery through which they were walking. To Karlo he said, "Flight of stairs ahead, then down to the left and two doors more." Karlo nodded, whispered hoarsely to Czarny, and then they were running down the stairs and into a lighted areaway that was vaulted overhead. From the guardroom came the noise of laughter, and they walked quietly ahead. Stooping so that he would not be seen over the half door of the guardroom, Karlo reached it and stood suddenly, covering the three guards inside with his pistol. One of them reached for a rifle, but Karlo fired at him and he screamed as the breath escaped his punctured lung, and then when he was on the floor Karlo shot him again, a little higher and through the heart. The other two guards were rigid with fright. When Czarny gave them an order, they quickly produced a ring of keys. Karlo took the keys, motioned to Webb, who pointed out the cell door, and then they were matching the key with the lock and trying each one, until the fourth key turned the big, old-fashioned lock, and the door opened inward.

In the darkness Webb could see nothing, but he remembered the bed against the left wall, and went to it, feeling with his hands in the half-light until his fingers touched an arm and he heard a moan. Karlo took the old man's feet, Webb his shoulders, and as they carried him out into the passageway, Webb saw Karlo drop Capska's feet quickly, and in the same instant there was the amplified sound of a pistol shot from the vaulted area and Czarny fell to the floor. From his knees Karlo sighted at the soldier who had come upon them, and Webb heard two quick *psst-pssst* sounds and the clatter of a rifle against marble. Karlo turned and fired at the two guards inside the room and they fell awkwardly against the chess table and the wall with the noise of a flatcar unloading. Karlo caught the old man's feet in his hands, and then the two of them were running through the vaulted area, past the body of the dead soldier who had shot Czarny through the back, up the stairs, and along the dark gallery that led to the corridor and the entrance by the guard boxes.

Webb's heart was hammering like a piston, and he held the old man's shoulders with weakening arms as they raced down the incline toward the graveled turnaround where Eduard was waiting in the car.

Behind them they could hear shouts and the clattering of heels on marble, but they plunged ahead until they were at the car and Webb was pushing the old man into the rear seat while Karlo grabbed the automatic weapon, threw a shell into the chamber, and sighted up the pathway at the volley of sounds. Before it was necessary to fire, Eduard had started the car with a jerk that forced Webb back against the springs of the rear seat, and Karlo's barrel slewed around crazily as he was thrown momentarily off balance.

Lights off, the car gathered speed down the hill, turning short at the road and heading west toward Ruzyne.

Beyond the city there was quietness, and without lights the road was a ribbon of moonlight winding inexorably ahead. Webb took the flask that Karlo gave him and tried to force liquor into Capska's mouth, but the teeth were set rigidly, and when the old man's eyes opened they glared wildly at Webb. Karlo turned and spoke anxiously in Slovak but Capska only shook his head. Then Karlo said to Webb, "He not believe he free. Think this only another STB trick."

In Spanish Webb said to Capska, "You're among friends, Dr. Capska. We're taking you from Prague to a place where you can be free." He could feel Capska's muscles begin to relax.

In slow Spanish, Capska said, "Who are you?"

"An American."

"And these other men?"

"Followers of yours."

"Where do we go now?"

"To Ruzyne."

The old man turned away. "Useless," he said. "They will stop us there."

Karlo broke in, gesturing with his hands, talking while he looked out of the rear window at the road behind. Webb saw Capska's face relax once more, felt the old man's thin hand on his wrist, reaching for the flask. Webb gave it to him, saw Capska tilt it back and swallow, then wipe his lips and give back the flask. "Good," Capska said in Spanish. "Very good, my young friend." He looked from Webb to Karlo and said, "Even if we do not escape, I will die happy in the knowledge that there are still brave men in my country." Karlo looked away respectfully, and brought up the automatic weapon between his knees. Webb took out his pistol, slipped off the safety, and said to Capska, "Can you walk, sir?"

His hands moved helplessly. "A little. A few meters, perhaps. No more. I am afraid you will have to help me."

Webb nodded. "I'm flying the plane," he said. "When we get in it, just sit back and close your eyes. If we get killed, it'll happen quickly."

Capska nodded. "I am old, but you will see that I am not afraid to die." He spoke to Eduard and Karlo, then again, in Spanish, to Webb. "Particularly in the company of brave men."

"No one ever doubted your bravery," Webb said, and from the corner of his eye he saw the beacon lights of Ruzyne sweeping across the sky.

Karlo pointed excitedly, and Webb leaned to one side and looked upward so that he could see the bright half-moon and the North Star. There was no time left to study his air charts; he would have to do that when they were airborne.

The car's right side lurched toward the shoulder and the wheels spun for a moment in dirt and gravel, then Eduard fought the car back onto the hard surface and said something to Karlo.

Even over the roar of the racing engine, Webb could hear the powerful thrust of a big plane's propellers pulling it along the runway for take-off. Automatically his hands moved imaginary throttles, pulled against the stick, and as he looked ahead, toward the airfield, he saw a three-engine plane lift off the end of the runway, its exhausts spitting red and purple behind it, its underbody illuminated briefly in the dying glow of the landing lights.

There was a fence ahead, marking a T intersection, and Eduard slowed to turn to the right. He slammed at the brakes, skidding the car toward the edge of the road, then let it edge downward into a cluster of foliage. Karlo kicked open one door as Eduard opened another, and Webb pushed Capska forward into Eduard's arms and got out beside the embankment. Eduard pulled Capska upward with Webb pushing behind, while Karlo covered them from the rear with his cocked machine gun. The fence, beyond the road, was only shoulder-high, and Webb went over it first to receive Capska as Eduard and Karlo boosted him across.

His arms around their shoulders, Webb and Eduard half carried, half pulled Capska along the dark edge of a runway until Karlo, twenty feet ahead of them, shouted something, and Eduard pointed to the right, where there was a faint red glow in the darkness. They pivoted toward it, running across the hard apron toward the signal light, and Webb felt that he must somehow force more air into his lungs if he were to make it all the way. He bit at the wind with his teeth, feeling his sand-dry mouth gulping in spasms. His legs were concrete weighted with cement.

Karlo was far ahead of them, shouting into the blackness, and from the red glow came an answering shout. Behind them a plane skimmed down the runway, its propellers tearing at their ears with their monstrous noise, deadening Webb's thoughts, leaving only the ultimate necessity of reaching the red light with the man whose arm was around his neck.

As they jogged nearer, Webb could see the outline of a small plane reflected in the glow of the signal light. He cursed disappointedly, for he recognized it as an old German training plane, a little larger than a Piper Cub, but with the same restricted range and slow flight characteristics. It was a miserable substitute for the bomber he had been promised. Shadows moved beside the plane, and there was the sound of its engine barking into life. A line of sparks shot from the double exhaust stack, and the little plane trembled from the pull of the turning prop.

Webb saw two men lift the tail of the plane and move it sideways so that the nose was heading toward the smooth apron behind them. Another man ran toward the four of them and pumped Karlo's hand. Webb's eyes searched the shadows for the girl he had prayed would be there, but he could see only the men and the plane, and the distant lights of the control tower beyond.

One of the men came up from the tail and opened the cabin door, holding it against the blast from the propeller. Webb ducked out from under Capska's arm and hurried toward Karlo. Shouting through the drone of the propeller, he said, "Where's Herta?"

Karlo looked at him and shook his head. "She could not come."

"Where is she?"

Karlo touched the arm of the man who had come out to greet him, said something, then looked back at Webb. "In Bratislava, American. She sent her love."

"Did she say anything else?"

Karlo looked at the other man, asked him a question, and came back to Webb. "There was not time," he said. "She had to leave Prague quickly."

Webb nodded, and looked toward the cabin door, where Capska was being helped inside. He said, "Is there gas enough for Linz?"

"There is gas for double the distance."

"What do I say when I land?"

"Ask for British Military Police. Tell them who your passenger is. There is nothing else."

Webb held out his hand and it was grasped by Karlo. "I'm sorry about Czarny," he said. "I won't forget him."

"We will not forget you, American," Karlo said, and stepped back, away from the rush of wind.

Before he climbed into the cabin, Webb looked for a moment at the circle of faces around him, at the small plane, quivering against its chocks, the lights of Ruzyne behind, and then with a gesture of his hand he said good-by to them and got quickly into the plane.

For a moment he studied the instruments, felt the stick and the rudder pedals, looked at the unfamiliar calibrations on the gauges, and pushed the throttle forward. He could see the men jerking the chocks away, and then he became a part of the vibrating plane that trundled over the rough ground toward the hard-surfaced apron, and as he strapped himself into the seat he half turned to see Capska behind him, sitting in the little seat, his face calm, his eyes open and interested in what Webb was doing.

Webb had estimated that the longest reach of the apron stretched away from the tower, and as he reached the black asphalt, he could see new lights by the fence over which they had come. He throttled full ahead, whipping around the tail, and the plane moved quickly down the runway, bobbing a little over surface irregularities, and he felt it respond to a slight motion of the stick. Without looking at the revolution indicator, he sensed when flying speed had been reached, pushed the nose down very slightly, then pulled the stick back into his lap.

The plane left the runway without straining, and as he looked below he saw the fence ahead into which he would have crashed in another five seconds. The compass showed northeast, and Webb turned the nose to the right, half circling over the end of the field, and from the darkness below there were sickening spurts of flame and beams from spotlights centered on the area he had just left.

His throat tightened again as he looked up from the field below toward the horizon, and steadied the compass on south. He held the plane in a gentle climb, and after ten minutes, when the lights of Prague were only flickering embers behind, he drew out the air charts, laid them across his knees, and began reading them in the light from the instrument panel.

As he flew, he scanned the dark sky above, below, and behind, looking for the telltale flares of exhaust stacks that would mean fighter planes had been sent to bring him down. Once he thought he saw lights pursuing him, but when his heart thawed again, he saw that they were only the afterglow of a falling star. He wanted desperately to think of nothing but flying the plane, of bringing it safely to Linz, but the events of the last six hours were too much with him to permit the peace of mind he craved.

The chart showed five thousand feet as a safe altitude, but Webb held the plane five hundred feet higher in case the altimeter had not been checked before takeoff. The course was, as Karlo had told him, almost due south. Because he was not in touch with either Prague or the Linz tower, he did not know the winds aloft, but he had decided that if he did not come into the Horsching airfield range at Linz within an hour more, he would have to begin search procedure that would finally pin-point the tower.

Holding the stick between his knees, he set the small radio on the Linz frequency, 137.88 megacycles, and listened to the comforting O-S-O-S signal that told him he was on the beam. The tanks were still nearly full, the plane did not seem to be drifting much, and in the clear moonlight Webb could see the reflection from streams and ponds below, stabbing up like silver blades.

When a running fix showed him west of Budejovice, he turned in on the DF station, fixed his position accurately, and tuned back to the Linz beam again. He noticed how clumsily his hands did things now, how long it took him to calculate simple mathematics, and he knew that he was very near to exhaustion. He said something to Capska, and when the old man did not answer he looked around and saw his chin resting comfortably on his chest. To make sure he was still alive, Webb touched him lightly and saw Capska's head begin to move. Webb looked back at the horizon, listened to the Linz signal growing in strength, and saw a railroad underneath that marked the Austrian border.

His shoulders slumped with relief, his breath came easily and regularly, and his heart stopped its pounding. Even if he were forced down now, they would be comparatively safe. The knowledge came to him as though from an unbelievable distance, and he pushed the throttle ahead for more speed, he felt cold tears trickling down his cheeks.

Using the Danube as a check point, he turned east toward the Horsching tower and followed the east-west beam directly over the airfield. A searchlight caught him, blinding him until he found the control-tower frequency and shouted at the tower controller to turn it off. Within thirty seconds the searchlight had turned away from him, and he was hearing landing instructions from a well-modulated English voice.

The field lighted up in a welcoming blaze, and as Webb throttled down toward the end of the apron, he realized how ridiculously small his plane must look to a controller accustomed to bringing in the big ones. An ambulance was drawn up at the flight line, just beyond the point where Webb pulled back and let the wheels drop to a three-point on the hard-faced runway. Then he was turning the plane toward the parking area, and people were running toward him from the base of the tower.

At first, when he saw their uniforms, the thought came to him that he had erred somehow, and been tricked into landing at Prague—that what he thought had been the Danube was only the Vltava—but the white British MP brassards told him his navigation had been correct, and that he and Jaro Capska were safe.

Whipping the tail around, he cut the engine, opened the door, and undid his safety belt. He was without strength to move, but he was lifted from the plane and supported on the ground while two husky soldiers brought out Capska. A British captain said to Webb, "And who might you be?"

"I'm an American," Webb said wearily. "Is there an odd type name Frean around here?"

"There certainly is," the captain said. "You'll be wanting to see him?"

"Right away."

"And so you shall. Now, how about the old gaffer with you?"

"He's quite a guy," Webb said. "Ask Frean about him." He felt himself being walked toward the administration building, and he was almost too tired to keep himself from stumbling. He saw Capska carried into the building on a stretcher and the door close behind him. All at once Webb felt sick and hollow, even though it was not yet completely over. Because he knew that it marked the end of his life as he had known it.

Drinking hot chocolate in Horace Frean's quarters, Webb said, "I left a couple of buddies behind me in Zürich. What became of them?"

Frean smiled slyly. "Bloody tragic it was," he said. "Loor hired a couple of ex-SS men to do them in." He looked at Webb. "If you'd seen the corpses with me, you'd agree it was money well spent."

Webb shook his head in mock sorrow. "All because of me, I suppose."

"Yes, laddie. All because of you."

When Webb spoke again he said, "I asked the girl to come with me, you might as well know. I tried to get her to come."

"It might have been a good idea, Kaspar. The stamp shop was raided last night."

"But she escaped?"

"Yes. She left Prague before the STB arrived."

"Have you heard from her?"

"Not yet. Maybe not for a week."

"How does she get word to you?"

Frean laughed and knocked the ashes from his pipe. "You'll never make a confidential agent, laddie. You ask too many questions."

"I'm serious," Webb said. "Capska was only part of this deal; the girl is the rest."

"You must be partial to families," Frean said casually. "She's the old man's daughter, you know."

"His daughter?" Webb repeated. "She never told me."

Frean patted him on the shoulder. "She must care for you, laddie. Otherwise, she'd have let you know she was the daughter of the man you'd helped give back to the Commies."

"She worshiped him," Webb said, "but I never thought of anything but hero worship."

"Maybe a bit of that, too." He looked at his watch and said, "You've had a rough go. How about a little sleep?"

Webb began taking off his shoes and asked, "Is Vienna far from here?"

"No. Not far."

"I'd like to go there."

"Any special reason?"

"Of course. Jaro Capska's daughter. How much longer do you think she can last there, alone?"

Frean shrugged. "Quite a while, probably. Then again, this last show may have done for her."

"That's what I was thinking."

"I see," Frean said. "So you want to go back."

"There's nothing for me anywhere else."

Frean said, "For Vienna you need a Russian permit."

"Can you arrange one?"

"Probably."

"Then do it."

"Look," Frean said. "If it should turn out that she's perfectly safe for the time being—that they aren't onto her at all—then what?"

"She'll have to decide," Webb said. "If she stays, then I stay, even though she has to hide me and feed me. I don't think she'll choose to endanger both of us."

Frean smiled slowly. "She told you how it would be."

"Yes."

"She told the truth," Frean said. "I could stop you, Kaspar. I could put you on a plane for New York and arrange to have you met at Idlewild."

"Then you'd be a son of a bitch," Webb said. "I've earned something from you, Frean. If you want to play God, go back to Zürich where there isn't so much competition."

Frean laughed merrily. "All right, laddie," he said. "You can walk to Bratislava from Vienna in a night—with luck."

"I'm lucky these days," Webb said. He lay back on the bed and closed his eyes. "Is her name Herta?"

"No. Karel."

"Karel," Webb repeated. "Karel Capska."

"She's a fine girl," Frean said. "Just don't risk her life."

"I'm not likely to," Webb said, "except bringing her out. Then, if anything goes wrong, at least we'll be together."

"Very noble," Frean said.

"You tire me. Maybe Kaspar can do something else for you before he comes back."

"Maybe," Frean said. "I'll let Kaspar know." He got up from his chair and walked to the door of the bedroom. "The express leaves at ten-twenty tomorrow. I'll have your ticket and permit."

"So long, buddy," Webb said. He reached up slowly, turned off the light, and heard Frean close the door. Sleep came to him almost at once.

CHAPTER ELEVEN

In Vienna, a one-legged boy with a crutch begged a cigarette from Webb at the Bahnhof, but Webb gave him some Czech koruny instead. The boy was no older then twelve, and his pinched face and crutch-distorted shoulder made him at once an object of pity to Webb.

In broken English the boy said, "Thanks, mister."

Webb walked toward the Bahnhof exit, the boy limping rapidly beside him. "You speak English?"

The boy nodded eagerly. "Little bit, mister. What you want to know?"

"A lot of things," Webb said. "Like a place to sleep."

"Very hard," the boy said, and pointed to a pile of rubble where workers were slowly sorting bricks from heaps of plaster. "Soldiers have all good hotels."

"A room, then."

The boy looked quizzically at Webb, balanced himself on his leg, and twirled his T-shaped crutch like a baton. "You can pay?"

"I've got a little money."

"Want to stay with girl?"

"No."

"Alone?"

"If possible," Webb said.

"I take you place," the boy said. The crutch halted parallel to the sidewalk, pointing at a taxi, and the cab pulled up beside them.

When they were inside, Webb asked, "What's your name?"

"Franz."

"Were you born here?"

"Vienna?"

Webb nodded.

"I think so. Yes. But on the other side of the Danube."

"Where do you live now?"

The boy shrugged and pointed at a pile of rubble.

"There is one place."

"And the others?"

"The same." The boy leaned forward, whispered to the driver, and leaned back again beside Webb. "Why you come to Vienna, mister? Stockings? Cigarettes?"

"Perhaps. Know anyone who'd like to buy?"

The boy nodded. "I bring him to you."

"Good," Webb said. He looked out of the cab window at a wrecking crew pulling down a brick wall. Beside the wall stood a newly built leather shop, its modernistic window crammed with luggage, letter folders, belts, and brief cases. A few cotton-stockinged women paused to look at the luxurious display; others hurried past with their market baskets.

He felt Franz touching his arm, and turned to look at him. The boy said, "What's your name, mister?"

"Williams," Webb said. "Call me Bill."

"Sure, Bill." The boy took one of the bank notes Webb had given him and looked at it. "You work for Russians?"

"Why?"

The boy shrugged. "Sometimes it is best to know."

"Well," Webb said, "I'm not working for anybody. I'm working for myself."

"Everybody works for someone," Franz said. "To have Czech money, you must work for someone."

"I found it," Webb said. "There was a purse on the floor of the train."

Franz looked at him suspiciously. "You been Vienna before?"

"No." Webb pointed toward the street. "Where are we? I mean what zone?"

Franz squinted through the window. "Russian."

"I don't want a room in the Russian Zone," Webb said. "We'll have to go somewhere else."

Quickly the boy called a number to the driver and said, "Moldaustrasse."

Webb could see the driver's head nod. The cab turned a corner and bumped over street car tracks, and Franz said, "British Zone now."

"That's better." Webb took a small chocolate bar from his handbag, broke it in two, and gave half to Franz. The boy did not eat the chocolate, but folded the wrapper around it carefully and placed it inside his shirt pocket. Webb asked, "Don't you like chocolate?"

The boy's thin lips said, "I love chocolate, mister."

"Then eat it."

Franz shook his head. "Why? I can sell it."

"Eat it," Webb ordered. He took another Czech bill from his pocket and gave it to the boy. "I'm buying it. For you."

Franz took the bill quickly, unwrapped the chocolate, and crammed it into his mouth. Webb said, "You're pretty thin for a kid your age. Got any folks?"

"Folks?"

"Mother? Father?"

"No. Only one sister."

"She lives in Vienna?"

"I think so."

"Don't you live with her?"

The boy swallowed the last of the chocolate and shook his head. "She want the bed," he said. "For men who stay there."

"I see," Webb said. He felt the taxi begin to slow, then pull to the curb in front of a shoddy façade of buildings. Franz said something to the driver, then spoke to Webb. "Five schillings," he said.

Webb took the schillings from his pocket, counted them into the driver's hand, and got out of the taxi. He held open the door for Franz, then closed it when the boy hopped onto the sidewalk, balancing himself with his crutch. Carrying his handbag, Webb walked toward the tall, scarred door where Franz had pointed. Most of the buildings on the street had escaped being destroyed by Russian artillery. A few doors away he could see the entrance to a night club, a lifeless neon tube forming the outline of a nude girl with a top hat and spike heels. Franz followed his glance and said, "Very good place, mister."

"How would you know?"

"My sister. She tell me."

Webb pulled a bell wire beside the door and heard the sound echo inside the building. Behind him the cab pulled away and chugged down the cobblestoned street. In the seconds that Webb waited before he heard heels descending a stone stairway inside, he began to feel afraid again; namelessly, without reason. Or was it because he was completely on his own? Was it because Frean's eyes had told him Frean never expected to see him alive again—that the forged permit, the schillings, the advice Frean had given him were wasted?

The door opened and an old woman peered up at him from a half crouch. Franz burst into a flow of German that Webb did not try to listen to. When it was over, the woman bowed half mockingly, and Webb stepped over the doorsill into a hallway lighted only by the circular stair shaft that spiraled upward to the broken skylight. He looked at the gray concrete stairway, then picked up Franz and began climbing the stairs. The woman followed behind them, talking under her breath, and occasionally Franz would answer her. Webb passed the first landing, then the second, and by the time he reached the third, the boy's eighty pounds seemed to have tripled.

The landing led to a short corridor with two doors, and while Webb waited for the woman to reach them he slowed his breathing and looked downward at the landing three stories below. The landlady reached the landing, puffing and talking to herself, and took a key from a round brass ring. She waddled toward the farthest door, put the key in the lock, and opened the door.

The room was darker than the hallway. The windows, overlooking an inside courtyard, were thick with a discolored soot that looked like a growth of fungus. There was a water basin, a single light bulb near the ceiling, and a closed closet door.

Franz took Webb's handbag, crutched to the closet, and dropped the bag inside, leaving the closet door ajar. The woman held out her hand, and Webb asked Franz, "How much?"

"Ten schillings."

Webb whistled softly and saw the smirk on the woman's face. He gave her the money and sat down on the vari-colored bed. The woman jingled the schillings into her dress pocket and backed out of the room, crouching like a toad. The door closed behind her, and Webb looked up at Franz. "So this is home," he said. "Is it safe?"

"From *Polizei*?"

Webb nodded.

"It is safe." Franz leaned against the washstand. "What do you want in Vienna?"

"Very little. A change of clothes, a knife, a flashlight, a map, and a compass."

"Which way do you go?"

"South," Webb lied.

"For cigarettes?"

"No. Swiss chocolate."

"You will take me?"

"I can't," Webb said. "I'll go too fast for you." He looked at the boy's heavy crutch, thick as the neck of a baseball bat; its T top, slightly concaved to fit the armpit.

"You know how to bring back this chocolate?"

"By truck," Webb said. "It comes by truck."

"I can help you sell it," Franz said.

"How would I find you?"

Franz twirled his crutch with one hand. "Ask at the Bahnhof for Franz," he said. "Franz with the crutch." He raised the wooden object as though to balance it, then Webb heard the floor creak behind him. As he tried to duck forward, to shield his head between his knees, he knew that his mistake had been in forgetting to look inside the closet, but even as the first blow landed on the side of his head, a silly hope flashed through his mind that the boy would be able to help him. Half twisting away from the pistol butt and the strange face of his attacker, Webb saw Franz lean forward and grasp the end of the crutch with both hands.

For an instant, Webb thought the crutch was aimed at the man with the pistol, but when he saw Franz's lips parted in a wolflike smile, he knew that the crutch was hurtling toward his own head. As he threw himself convulsively forward in a last effort to escape their blows, he wondered which would strike him first. Then, in the next split instant, the flash of blinding pain that seared his brain numbed him to the blow that followed.

Wearily, as though he were climbing a spiral staircase with a truck on his back, Webb forced himself upward toward light that seemed to come from a distant broken skylight. He had forgotten how to breathe; his lungs had lost their function—atrophied into dried, stiff codfish—in the ages since he had used them. Breathing again brought pain. Pain brought semiconsciousness and the ability to open his eyes. At first he thought he was staked out in the desert sun, but as his eyes cleared, the sun became a light bulb; the sand, a hard floor under his body. His hand touched the back of his head and felt something like warm, half-set gelatin. He looked at his fingers' oxblood color, and felt sick. The pain circled his head like a crushing serpent against which he had no defense. Too weak to rise, he turned his head and threw up where he lay. The vomit ran alongside his arm, and he closed his eyes again.

All at once, it seemed, his mind began to function, closing the gaps in his memory, telling him he'd been tricked like a farm boy in Chicago. Lured to a pad joint and mugged. He forced himself to sit up, and the pain beat against his forehead like the pistons of a steam calliope. Clutching the bedclothes, he dragged himself sideways until he was half lying across the edge of the bed. His mind had lost all sense of time. How long had he been there? A week? A day? A month?

He felt his wrist, but his watch was gone. As he stumbled upright he missed the half-expected sound of coins in his pocket. When he looked at his thighs, he saw that his pockets were turned inside out. His coat had been knifed open and the wallet extracted through the slit over his right breast. He turned toward the closet where his handbag had been placed, but it was gone too; taken by the kid he had pitied and his accomplice.

Cold tap water gurgled reluctantly, then flowed in splashing profusion. Webb tore off a soiled pillowcase, sopped it in the washbasin, and wound it around his face and head. Thin, knifelike pain slashed through him from his lacerated scalp. It seemed to play around the frings of the steady, monotonous pain that penetrated his brain like a driven stake.

When he could stand the cold compress no longer, he threw the bloodied pillowcase to the floor, dried his face on a sheet, and gingerly combed his hair with his fingers. Because his wallet was gone, his permits were gone, too. And his money. He looked around the filthy room, disgusted with himself. He had paid the old witch ten schillings, but he did not know if it was for a night or a week. Without his gray permit, he could not go to the police. Without money, he was trapped where he was. Webb cursed, and felt himself shake with anger.

The key was inside the door, and Webb took it with him when he went out. He held onto the rail, walking down the stairs, and when he was at the bottom he walked through the dark entrance and out onto the street, and blinked at the crude outline of the nude dancer, haloed in sputtering red neon. A taxi turned the corner, and Webb shrank into the shadows. The cab stopped in front of the night club's neon sign and two well-dressed couples got out. The sound of their laughter infuriated him. He was desperate now, with an overwhelming urge to regain what had been stolen from him. Without half thinking, he knew that to get money with which to buy what he needed for his journey, he would get it the way it had been taken from him. His eyes searching, his mind alert once more, he turned from the night club and walked down the street.

In a rubble pile nearly two blocks away he found what he wanted—a short length of iron pipe. The rust twisted off in flakes against his hand as Webb shoved it into the pocket of his torn coat. Walking back toward the night club, he wrapped his handkerchief around the business end of the pipe, held it in his left hand, and picked up a stone lying near the curb. From the shadows of a doorway he threw it at the sign, but missed. Then he took a handful of smaller stones and hurled them with buckshot force in the direction of the neon light. The light tinkled out and blue sparks played around in the darkness for a moment before vanishing.

The street was totally dark.

Webb walked away from the scene of his sabotage, looking at the moon, to figure that the time was after midnight. The doorman would try to repair the sign; then he would give up, and no more patrons would come into the club. Without the after-midnight trade, the club would close earlier than usual, and the patrons would have to walk down the dark street before they could find a lighted street and taxis. Webb went back to his rubble pile, moved a few bricks to make a seat for himself, and lay back against comparatively soft broken plaster. He looked at the moon under which he had been flying last night, closed his eyes, and forced himself to doze.

When the moon had moved ten degrees, Webb got up stiffly, felt his iron pipe in his pocket, and walked slowly back toward the night club. His eyes were well adjusted to the darkness, and as he moved close to the buildings he saw and heard a couple leave the night club. They walked in the other direction, their heels scraping quickly over the sidewalk; a man and a woman. Webb shook his head. He could not afford an uproar when he struck. His prey would have to be alone. That narrowed his chance, for the average man did not go alone to a night club. Or if he went alone, he left with a woman. Thinking about it that way, Webb realized how greatly against him the chances were stacked, and the edge began to wear off his determination. If he could have thought of an alternative, he would have dropped the iron pipe and climbed the stairs to his room and slept. But there was nothing else he could do. There was no Traveler's Aid he could borrow from, no Salvation Army where he could find a coat, a knife, a map, and a compass.

Two more couples came out of the night club, then a long silence, and the sound of men's voices. Apparently the doorman was saying good night to an important customer. The talking got on Webb's nerves, and he cursed them for their talkativeness; but then, he did not blame the customer for not wanting to be left alone on the dark street. Finally the good nights were said, and, whistling, the customer turned and began walking toward Webb.

Webb clung to the doorway, holding his breath until the man had passed, walking slowly while his eyes adjusted themselves to the darkness. On tiptoe Webb followed, and beside the rubble pile he overtook his quarry. The iron pipe traveled half an arm's length against the back of the man's head, sopping him first under the brim of his felt hat. Webb caught him as he fell. Holding the man by the shoulders, feeling his own head pound from the pain of his exertion, Webb dragged him into the angle of two half-destroyed walls, hearing the rubble clatter apart like mortar explosions. Webb felt the man's heart beating as he took out his wallet, then opened the leather envelope and let his thumb riffle over the thick wad of schilling notes. With the man's folded hat, he made a pillow for the man's head and left him lying there, propped awkwardly against the uneven contours of the hard debris.

The iron pipe in his coat pocket, the stolen wallet in his trousers, Webb walked back to the building on Moldaustrasse where he had been robbed, pushed open the door, and walked quietly up the three flights to his room.

Before he turned off the light, he pushed his bed against the door, locked the windows, and laid the iron pipe on a chair close to his pillow. Then he buttoned the stolen wallet into his hip pocket and turned off the light. In five minutes he was asleep.

When he woke, he figured it must be after ten. He felt filthy, tired, and hungry. Before he left the room, he opened one of the grimy windows, threw the key outside, and closed the window. Then he went out of the room, letting the lock snap shut behind him.

At a newsstand he bought a map of Vienna. As he walked toward the Ringstrasse in the center of town he passed a coffee shop, and he stopped and went inside. The half-page menu was greasy and curled, its listings in blue ditto ink. Pointing to the menu, he ordered chocolate and rolls from the waiter, and wolfed them down when they came. He paid for his breakfast from the stolen wallet, studied the map a few moments longer, and noted the street that marked the division between the International Zone and the Russian Zone. Then he got up from the table and went out to the street again.

Three blocks farther and he saw a physician's brass sign being polished by a servant. Webb turned into the open doorway and walked up the flight of stairs to the doctor's office. There was no one in the outer room, so Webb pounded on the door of the examining room. In a moment the door opened and a short, fat man came out, pulling a long white coat over his street clothes. To his questions in German, Webb turned and pointed at the back of his head, where the hair was matted with dried blood. There was another bruise over his right temple, but the flesh had only been bruised, not broken, and Webb supposed the lump would go away in time. He followed the doctor into a white-enamel room, sat on a metal chair, and watched the doctor scrub.

The doctor cut away the hair from a patch the size of a small saucer, washed the laceration with alcohol, and injected a local anesthetic into Webb's scalp. Then the little man sterilized some black silk thread and a hooked needle and began sewing the lips of the wound together. Because of the anesthetic, Webb could feel no pain; only the pressure of the needle, the scrape of the thread through his torn scalp, like the vibration of a fingernail over canvas. The wound was sterilized again with a vile-smelling white powder, and a round bandage applied. When the doctor had finished, Webb handed him a sheaf of schilling notes, and when the doctor had selected three, Webb added another, said, "*Danke schön*," and went down to the street.

At a cheap store he bought a narrow-brimmed Tyrolean hat and put it on to hide the bandage. Then he found a barbershop and got a shave and a mustache trim. As he walked farther toward the Ring, he noticed dun-colored recon cars driven by the International Patrol pass by occasionally. Viennese policemen in their tall shakos directed traffic at the street crossings, and finally Webb found a store that sold sporting goods.

He bought a small, belt-size rucksack, a compass, a length of rope, a pair of heavy climbing shoes with rubber cleats on the soles, and long wool stockings. He saw a horn-handled knife with a thin blade and a sheath. The blade cut a piece of paper as though it were water, and Webb bought it. He put the rucksack on his belt, changed into the new stockings and shoes, and buttoned the knife and compass inside the rucksack. At a hardware store he bought a pair of carbon-hardened wire-cutters and a 9-mm. Steyr pistol, the size of a Colt .45.

A stationery store sold him a map that covered a fifty-mile radius around Vienna and indicated the crossings of the Danube between Vienna and Bratislava. Frean had told him of the trail to Grossenzersdorf, after which he must take to the fields to pass between Orth and Leopoldsdorf. The Danube was to be crossed at the fork north-northeast of Hainburg, and he was to keep just south of the hills beyond the river and follow the Danube to Bratislava.

The anesthetic in his scalp began to wear off, and he became aware of a tight, drawing pain from his wound. But with the knife and the pistol in his rucksack, he did not mind the pain. A certain optimism returned to him, and as he bought a suit of heavy, secondhand clothes, he found himself whistling. The coat was roomy enough to conceal the bag at his belt. Looking in the mirror, he saw himself as a middle-class Austrian sporting enthusiast; his bruised face even gave evidence of a recent climbing fall.

Hungry again, he ate at a cheap restaurant: pork, boiled potatoes, turnips, and cabbage. It was heavy food that would stay with him. For a few schillings more, the waiter brought a stone mug of warm milk, and while Webb drank it he made his plans.

A new watch strapped around his wrist, Webb got up from the park bench and walked down the Kartnerstrasse, beyond the Ring, toward the east. The time was two o'clock.

A block away he bought half a dozen bars of milk chocolate, grimaced wryly at the thought of the chocolate he had given Franz, and began eating one of the bars. Across the street was the Russian Kommandatura, a huge metal red star over the doorway. Sloppily dressed boy soldiers guarded the entrance. Hung against the building's second story were two story-long portraits: Lenin and Stalin. Webb spat at the street, and moved on. A Russian jeep pulled up in front of the Kommandatura, and three soldiers hurried inside. It reminded him of the way he had gone into Hradcany Castle two nights ago, and he felt a sick longing for the company of Karlo, Eduard, and Czarny. The red hammer-and-sickle banner waved in the afternoon breeze, and the portraits of Lenin and Stalin billowed and sank back.

Webb bought a copy of *Der Tageblatt,* feeling it was good insurance to be seen carrying the paper, rolled it into a cylinder, and carried it under his arm. If he were stopped suddenly, he could use it as a temporary weapon to slash downward at a pistol or forward at a man's face.

His clothing was too warm for a summer afternoon when Viennese men were wearing *lederhosen* and short-sleeved shirts, but he could not take off his coat without revealing the rucksack at his belt, and the heavy clothing's warmth would be necessary during the night.

He walked slowly toward the Danube, sauntering disinterestedly with the crowd of Austrians and occupation soldiers, and when he reached the river he saw that the bridge was two blocks away. Webb found a bench along the embankment, unrolled his newspaper, and pretended to read. As he watched the bridge, he saw Russian guards stop a truck or a cab occasionally and poke their fingers against market baskets. He had to cross the river, but he was afraid to go by cab or streetcar, where his unfamiliarity with the fare and his inability to speak a few German words would mark him as a foreigner. If he walked alone, he was sure something in his gait would make him seem different from other Austrians, walking beside him.

Webb waited.

In fifteen minutes he was acutely uncomfortable; his mouth was dry, his palms were slick with sweat. Then, in the distance, he could hear the tinny sound of a small brass band coming toward the Danube. Webb saw other people standing around the corner, looking expectantly toward the sound of the martial music, and he got up and walked over to them.

Policemen had halted traffic, and Webb could see files of children wearing red brassards, marching to the comic-opera music. A color guard of boys carried the red-white Soviet banner well in front of the platoons of marching boys and girls. It was a Communist Youth parade.

Webb waited tensely while the parade grew nearer, then began walking slowly along the sidewalk, flanking a platoon of young girls, none of whom were over ten or eleven. Other men and women were walking parallel to Webb, in the street and on the sidewalk—the parents of the parading children. The parade headed directly for the bridge, and as he stepped onto the apron of the bridge, Webb began to applaud and cheer loudly with the children's parents. His head turned toward the children, his hands clapping, his voice growing hoarse with shouting, Webb walked over the bridge in the center of a group of proud Austrian parents, past the bored Russian guards. He walked two blocks farther with the parade, then stopped, as though to tie his shoe, and stepped down a small side street, away from the noise and the marchers.

His coat was stifling him in the midafternoon heat, and he took it off, tucking the neck inside his trousers at the back, so that the rucksack was concealed. He shooed away some sparrows from a drinking fountain, splashed water against his face, and drank from his cupped hands. With his shirt sleeve he wiped the water from his face, and he saw in the distance the high, slowly revolving ferris wheel that marked the Prater.

Webb was alone in the Soviet Zone.

From memory, he found the street that ended in the path to Grossenzersdorf, and timed his pace against the second hand of his wrist watch. He had about thirty miles to travel and slightly more than five hours of daylight remained. At a steady four miles an hour, he would be at Hainburg by nightfall, and the border was two miles farther—another half hour's walk. But Webb did not want to cross the border until perhaps two o'clock—the darkest hour in this phase of the moon. That meant a delay of six hours along the route; slower time on the hills and through the woods would lengthen his walking time another two hours, giving him probably four hours when he could try to rest before crossing the border.

It was more time than he had counted on.

No matter how he argued it, there was no reason not to travel to a point west of Hainburg by daylight. The hike would harden him for the more difficult going at night. The head start by day gave him a chance to rest a few hours at night. Webb found an angle intersection and bore to the right without looking at his map.

Here the houses and shops were not built together in a single façade; instead they were grouped in twos and threes, and when he had gone another mile, the pavement showed masses of chuckholes, then gave way entirely to hard-packed clay that followed the edges of a narrow pond. The clay was easier on his feet, encased as they were in heavy new shoes. The thick rubber cleats on his soles raised little whorls of dust, and as he turned to look back at Vienna, he could see dust suspended above his trail. In the distance he could see the tall, thin spire of St. Stephen's Church standing high above the bombed roofs of Vienna. He raised his hand in a mock salute to the distant city and said, "I heard you were a lovely lady, but by the time I got to know you, you were only a toothless old whore."

Then he turned and fished out his prismatic compass as he walked to the east, checked his course, and slipped the safety off his pistol.

In the low land of the Danube valley the going was easy; his only handicap was thirst. Before he reached Grossenzersdorf he crossed a little creek that fed into the river, and he drank from it. He soaked his Tyrolean hat in the creek, wrung it out a little, and put it back on his head. The water's evaporation cooled the top of his head, easing the pain of his stitched wound.

He could see farmers cultivating the soil, helped by women and young girls. The farms were laid out neatly, and where there were no crops, there were cattle grazing in the sun, the calves asleep in the shade of orchard trees. Fatigue was beginning to gnaw at his thighs now. Once he saw a trail of dust raised by a car on another road, and watched it until he saw it was not coming toward him. He paused and wiped his forehead, for it had been a Russian vehicle.

Once he passed a German tank, resting where it had been destroyed, at the edge of a field. The tracks peeled grotesquely away from the wheels like macabre jungle leaves; the muzzle of the gun was blown back in strips like the petals of a long-stemmed flower. The black Nazi cross had almost weathered off the turret, and the once brown paint was blistered and flaking. When the field had been plowed and planted in the spring, the farmer had narrowed in straight lines until he reached the tank's jutting outline. Then the harrow had been diverted in a curve around the tank, and now wheat grew within a few feet of the rusting metal, almost as high as the long, low body.

The war of which that tank had been an instrument was almost as far from Webb's mind as the First World War, and the issues that had been involved seemed unimportant now. Ahead of him, somewhere beyond the outline of the hills, at a slow-moving stretch of the Danube, lay a town under Russian occupation, where the girl he loved lived a double life. Behind him, he could feel the sun beginning to lower at last; its rays did not seem to pierce his back like nails. Instead, a light afternoon breeze sprang up, bringing with it some coolness from the nearby Danube. Webb hitched up the clawing weight at his belt and dug his heels into the surface of the road.

CHAPTER TWELVE

WAKING SUDDENLY, he threw out his arm instinctively, striking his wrist against the bole of a tree. He was half sitting, half lying against the tree, his pistol in his lap, and his right hand closed round the pistol butt as he held his breath and listened in the darkness.

When he had convinced himself that he had heard nothing, he looked at the radium dial on his wrist and saw that the time was a little after one o'clock. He took his hand away from the pistol, shifted his position against the tree, and closed his eyes again. He had come to this wooded rise near the Danube about ten o'clock, eaten a chocolate bar, and fallen asleep. Now, according to his calculations, he was only four or five miles west of Bratislava, within a half hour of the Czech border. The silence of the woods reassured him, and he felt his body relax. The night had turned cold and his heavy coat was buttoned to the neck. His hands and legs were stiff, but three hours' sleep had rested him, driven away the exhaustion that had threatened him earlier. The rucksack dug into his lap, and he pushed it farther along his belt to a point where the wire-cutters did not dig into him. The knife in its sheath was strung on his belt beside his hand, and the feel of the cold horn handle gave him a sensation of security.

Under his legs the soft matting of pine needles insulated him from the colder ground, and he felt himself beginning to fall asleep once more. The thought that he would reach the little store beside St. Michael's gate by daylight gave him a pleasant feeling that seemed to warm him against the cold night air.

He thought about Karel Capska, what he would say to her; the plans they would make, the decisions ahead of them. Then, like a cloud across the moon, came a memory that forced itself into the twisted body of Nelda lying grotesquely in its last posture. Webb fought away the scene, thought of the long hike behind him, the dust, the thirst, and the fatigue, and then, before he realized it, he was asleep again.

The sound of a man's voice awakened him, and as he reached instinctively for the pistol, the light of an electric torch blinded his eyes and a sharp command brought him slowly to his feet. Webb raised his hand above his head, saw a soldier bend forward into the arc of light and pick up Webb's pistol. From the darkness behind the torch came the menacing growl of a dog. Webb could not see the animal, but he could imagine it poised to spring at this throat.

Sleep had gone; fatigue vanished. Blood pounded through his veins like the surging of an open sluice gate. In front of him there was nothing visible but the round, staring light. He heard two men talking in an unfamiliar language, saw the arm of one pointing at him, then a bayoneted rifle was leveled at Webb's stomach. One of the two soldiers stepped forward and began to search Webb. That meant the one with the torch was holding the rifle, too.

The searching soldier had been patting Webb's coat pockets; now he prodded Webb to turn from the light, and as Webb shifted his feet he dropped to his knees suddenly, rolling powerfully backward so that his arms windmilled against the unarmed soldier. Dropping to his belly, Webb kicked this body convulsively away from the zone of light, and saw the struck soldier stagger backward and collide against the flashlight. The light dropped to the pine-needle floor, rolled a few feet, and stopped, lighting a dark wall of trees.

The two soldiers were on the ground struggling to get up when the dog, acting on instinct, sprang out of the darkness at

Webb. The dog's fangs tore past his neck, grazing the skin, as Webb's hand fumbled for the knife at his belt. He was aware of the soldiers' rising to their knees as the dog whirled and sprang again. But this time Webb ducked to one side, and the dog impaled its belly on Webb's waiting knife. The animal shrieked with pain and clamped its jaws around Webb's upper arm. Even the heavy cloth was no protection against the animal's crushing jaws, and Webb felt his flesh tear as the dog's body slid to the ground.

He heard the snick of a rifle bolt and dove, for the flashlight. Belly to the ground, he arched his back and flung the flashlight into the forest. Then he rolled aside and heard the sharp crack of the rifle; pine needles and bits of dirt sprayed against his face.

With bent knees Webb half circled the open space where he had slept, hearing the dog's dying whimpers, the guttural voices of the soldiers. As he walked, stooping like an Indian, his foot encountered something hard, and his left hand touched it eagerly—the Steyr pistol.

Somewhere within a ten-foot radius the two soldiers, standing side by side, were listening for him. Reaching for his hip, Webb undid the rucksack, took out the heavy wire-cutters, and tossed them against a nearby tree. The muzzle flash of the rifle limned two white-faced soldiers, and Webb shot at them from the hip. The man with the rifle screamed and fell forward, the other whirled in terror and began to run through the underbrush.

Behind him, on the ground, the dog was still crying, and Webb knelt to put the pistol barrel against its head. The report of the pistol seemed to fill the forest and reverberate back to the little hill where Webb had slept. The animal twitched convulsively and lay still, the Steyr muzzle was wet with something that Webb rubbed off against his trouser leg. His right bicep was beginning to pain him; his head throbbed; his mind was filled with rage and a lust to kill the other soldier.

His hat was still lying at the base of the tree where he had used it as a pillow. Webb picked it up, unfolded it, and put it on his head. Then he bent over the body of the dead soldier and dragged it out of the clearing and into the underbrush. Holding the rifle like a javelin, he pitched it into the woods behind him. Then he caught hold of the dog's collar, pulled the warm carcass to the other side of the clearing, and kicked it down the hill.

The sound of breaking underbrush in the distance told him that the soldier was still running away. Webb took out his compass, took a bearing on the sound, and found that the soldier was heading east. Webb could trail him without losing time in doubling back. He put his knife into the sheath at his belt, decided against looking for the flashlight, and walked down the hill toward the sound of the fleeing man.

If there were a border garrison nearby, the shooting would have been overheard, but the garrison's search would probably be to the west. The guards would be used to searching for people escaping from Czechoslovakia, but they would be slow to comprehend the novelty of an illegal entry from the west.

Webb tried to follow the soldier's trail by watching for the white ends of broken branches, but the moon had almost failed, and in a few minutes he had to rely on sound alone to tell him the direction of the escaping soldier. Now that he was calmer he realized that he should have started after the soldier at once instead of bothering to hide the two bodies. If the soldier reached his companions, they could concentrate on searching for Webb; but if Webb could dispose of the second soldier, then the garrison would spend the night looking for two missing men, since they could not know that a third man had been involved in the sound of shooting.

His knees were blocked by a branch and he catapulted forward, barely turning the pistol muzzle away from the ground. The fall wrenched his bleeding arm and tore at the wound in his scalp, but Webb did not waste time cursing the branch. Instead, he picked himself up, blew at the pistol muzzle to clear it of earth and twigs, clenched his teeth against the pain of his body, and pushed ahead through the underbrush.

After another hundred yards he realized that he would not be able to overtake the soldier by following him through the woods, and that the ground was clearer toward the river. Still listening to the sounds ahead of him, Webb turned to the right and began to move toward the distant Danube, glistening sluggishly under the dying moon. After twenty yards he broke into a clearing and began to double-time along a course parallel to the sound of the running soldier. As he neared the source of the sounds, he could hear an occasional half-hysterical sob that made his pistol hand itch. His breath came pantingly and he knew that he could not keep up the exertion much longer. He would have to strike while he still had strength and steadiness enough to make sure of the kill. His watch showed ten minutes after two, and as he looked up from it, the light of the moon died away completely. He slowed his pace at once, trying to stifle the gasping of his lungs, and the thought came to him that he was within a few minutes of crossing the border into Czechoslovakia.

Bearing toward a knoll, Webb climbed it and looked toward the river, hoping to see the yoke-shaped confluence where he was to cross, but a sound ahead and to his left made him look quickly toward the woods and he forgot about the Danube. The sound had been so close that it startled him; evidently the soldier had stopped to rest or take his bearings. Webb moved softly over the ground until he reached the edge of the woods. Walking parallel to the trees, still heading east, Webb listened to the slow movements of the soldier among the trees. Then, suddenly, he saw the orange flame of a match illuminate briefly the face of a man, and then the match went out. Under his breath Webb cursed. He had not had time even to bring up his pistol, and he did not think the soldier would be striking many more matches. Without thinking, Webb began to run forward so that he would be parallel with the soldier blundering through the forest. If Webb tried to go back into the woods now, he would be heard. The land was sloping now down toward the bed of the Danube, and the foliage would have to end soon. Then, when there were no trees between him and the soldier, Webb could get close enough to kill the man.

If the soldier did not already know where he was, he would surely find a landmark when he came to the edge of the woods. Then his course would be directly toward the garrison hut, and each second from that time on would increase Webb's danger. He heard the soldier trip and fall heavily. Webb picked up a rock and threw it into the woods behind the desperate man. The rock crashed into the underbrush, and the soldier sobbed again and began running once more. Without light the soldier must be taking terrific punishment against the trees, Webb thought but the picture did not move him. Instead, he threw a heavier rock toward the sound of the panting soldier, heard it land, and then there were no more sounds until he heard the click of a pistol's slide snapping a cartridge into the chamber.

Webb stopped and went down on one knee. He had not thought the soldier would carry a side arm, but the sound of the pistol had warned him. The soldier's chances were much better now. In fact, Webb thought, if he were really smart, he would fire a few rounds to signal the garrison for assistance, but Webb knew that the soldier thought of himself only as a pursued man. Taking the offensive and calling for help or stalking Webb would probably not occur to him.

Beside him was the stump of a tree, and Webb got up and moved onto it. Listening for the soldier's next sound. Webb held the pistol ready to fire in his right hand, and with his left hand dug out his compass and oriented himself. His wrist watch told him that it was an hour and a half until dawn. By the time the sky began to turn gray he had to be across the river and at the outskirts of Bratislava.

Looking at his wrist watch, he realized that he had not heard the soldier for ten minutes; and that the soldier was probably sitting just as he was, waiting for a sound from Webb. That meant the man had mastered his hysteria and was beginning to think rationally. If the soldier heard a search party he would be calm enough now to signal his position and wait. Then Webb would have to break and run toward the river. By now, if all had gone well, the soldier would have been killed, and Webb would be rowing or floating across the Danube. But the unpredictable had happened, and now two men were sitting within a hundred feet of one another, each waiting for a movement or a noise that would show him where to fire.

Fifteen minutes more, and Webb's body was aching so throbbingly that he could stand it no longer. To break the impasse he moved off the stump and began crawling slowly on his hands and knees in the direction of the river. Twigs and stones tore at his palms and bruised his knees, but his progress was silent. When he came to the edge of a narrow creek, he paused long enough to drink and bathe his face, then crawled on.

After a while he rose painfully to his feet, massaged his stiffening right arm, and stumbled against a thicket he had not seen. He listened behind him for a moment, then tore himself loose and plunged ahead toward the river. He had wasted too much time trailing the soldier, and now he had to make it up as best he could. The stars stood out against the lightening sky, and as he looked to the east, a thin scimitar of gray showed on the horizon.

He lay beside the Danube, resting a few minutes before climbing down the bank and looking for a boat or a log. The bank was high at this point, so the river below was swift and deep. But he should have known that here, at the Y fork, the flow of water would change and become turbulent.

There was enough early light so that he could find his way down the moist clay bank without falling, but not so much that he could be seen from the other side as a well-defined target. He supposed that the other soldier must have turned back by now, and that the garrison would be alerted within a few minutes. He had had bad luck during the night; he deserved better luck now. He deserved, for instance, to find a driftwood-snagged boat or a children's raft, or a fisherman whose boat he could steal. As he walked along the shore, a few feet from the lapping water, he stumbled from weakness and began to laugh. He laughed involuntarily, thinking of the man in Vienna whose wallet he had stolen; of Franz and the lethal crutch; of Heinz and Gutierrez, who had been liquidated; of a toad of a man named Loor, who was perhaps behind federal bars; of Czarny and Karlo and Eduard, who had been killed while he made his escape; of a rotting corpse that had been Nelda; of little dead Ferdy. His laughter grew louder, until it pealed across the water and echoed back at him, muffled by the early river mist, and for a few moments he felt as though he had drunk a long shot of smoke. But as he calmed himself, forced himself to think of reality, he knew that only the poison of fatigue was destroying him.

When he could walk no farther, he leaned back against the bank and tried to breathe slowly and regularly. Mud had caught in the cleats of his soles, weighting down his feet, and as he scraped them clean he saw that his suit was snagged and torn in a dozen places. Dried blood caked the upper right arm of his coat, and briers and twigs had caught in his trousers.

Kneeling beside the river, he bathed his tooth-torn arm, shivering a little as he saw the red and purple lacerations where the guard dog had slashed him before he died. Then he rolled down his sleeve and put on his coat again. In the growing light he could see a shed a hundred yards ahead at the water's edge, the dim outline of a skiff snubbed at a nearby piling.

Walking close to the bank, Webb approached the shed from the shore, looked into the open window, saw no one, and waded a few feet out into the river after the boat. He was fumbling with the water-soaked knot at the piling when he heard a hoarse command, and looked up quickly to see a hatless soldier standing on the rim of the bank, pointing a pistol at him. The soldier said something else, and Webb raised his hands. He felt ridiculous standing knee-deep in water, but the sight of the soldier in the torn overcoat fifteen feet above him made his heart pound leadenly. As the two men faced each other without speaking, Webb felt utterly hollow and defeated. Clearly this meeting was only a mischance; the soldier, fearing punishment, had decided to desert and cross the Danube. So their paths had inevitably converged at the boathouse.

The soldier said something angrily, and motioned Webb to climb up toward him. For no reason he could analyze, Webb came slowly forward, limping heavily as though his right leg were badly injured. As he reached the shore again, he limped exaggeratedly, lurched toward the bank, and began clawing his way upward, slipping, digging the toe of his left foot into the soft clay, and moaning under his breath. He made hard work of it, so that when he was close to the edge, he looked up, panting hard, and saw a cruel smile of triumph on the soldier's face. Webb did not think the man was more than twenty-three or – four; and he was stockily built. A red star was implanted deep in the material of each uniform coat lapel, and Webb could see the pistol follow the movements of his head.

Dropping his eyes, Webb made a futile attempt to lift his left leg over the edge, but failed. He rested for a moment, his arms shielding his head, then tried again. This time his body cleared the edge completely and lurched awkwardly forward, and his right hand hooked around the soldier's heel and jerked back. The pistol exploded somewhere near Webb's head, but he pulled frantically and felt himself lose balance. He fell backward, rolled part way down the bank, and hit the shore at the edge of the water. The soldier clawed desperately at the bank to stop his downward motion, but then his body folded like a jacknife, and he landed on his knees beside Webb.

Webb was on his feet first, trying to rabbit-punch the soldier, but the man's overcoat collar protected the back of his neck, and he rolled sideways. A heavy boot kicked Webb's thigh, spinning him around in the slippery mud, overbalancing him near the piling beside the rowboat. Then the soldier was running toward the bank, searching for his pistol, and Webb moved toward him crazily, pulling the man backward toward the water, sensing that in the water the more lightly clad man would have the advantage. Their feet slipping from under them, their arms flailing, the two men fought at the water's edge. Then Webb kicked viciously at the back of the other's knees, buckling them, and as the man fell backward Webb caught him around the throat and dragged him into the water. The soldier's boots kicked themselves into the mud, trying to halt his backward motion, but the boots slid out of the thick mud with little sucking sounds.

When he was waist-deep in the river, Webb tightened his arm around the soldier's throat and forced his head underwater. The man's body was electrified, twisting, turning, clawing at Webb's wrists, insanely seeking leverage against which he could fight the death that was coming over him. Sobbing, Webb bent his knees, forced his legs apart to get purchase on the smooth river bottom, and tightened his grip around the soldier's throat with both his forearms. In his half crouch, water licked at his chin and the current tugged at his body, but his arms held their grip as though turned to concrete.

A bubble burst the surface of the water beside Webb's face, and the dying body in one terrible paroxysm almost wrenched itself free of Webb's crushing arms. But Webb managed to recover his grip, and the struggles weakly ceased.

Still holding the dead thing underwater, Webb blacked out. When he opened his eyes again, he was a few feet farther away from the rowboat, and the body had escaped his arms. He struck out toward the piling, hauled himself laboriously into the boat, and freed his belt knife from its sheath. He sawed at the wet rope until it parted, then put the single oar in the oarlock and began to scull the boat toward the opposite shore. It was hard, painful work to keep the bow pointed at the other bank, and the air was a clear gray now, and he knew that he could be seen from shore.

When he was in midstream, fighting the tide, Webb realized that the soldier's body, weighted down by the overcoat, would not rise for days; that even if he should be caught now, there would be nothing to connect him with the body of a strangled and drowned deserter.

Now that the heat of his struggle was over, his wet clothing, exposed to the river wind, began to chill him. Webb tried to lie below the gunwales, out of the wind, but he could not handle the oar with his injured right arm, and had to sit up again. The river was carrying him downstream at about ten knots, which would bring him to the other side at a point out of sight of the little shed where he had fought for his life.

Instead of trying to scull, Webb began using the oar as a rudder, pointing the bow into the tide, and saw that he was making almost as good progress as before. He put the oar handle under his left arm, held it close to his side, and hugged himself with both arms to try to save what little warmth remained in his body.

Twenty minutes more, and Webb had maneuvered the skiff into the shallows on the Czech side, and before he had time to put up the oar the bow had grounded on a mud flat. There was less than a foot of water where Webb stepped out of the boat, and he put the oar along the bottom and pushed the bow free of the mud with his foot. Caught by the current, the skiff bobbed toward the center of the river, gaining speed as it drew out of sight behind a spit of land.

His teeth chattering, Webb dragged himself up the low bank and into a wheat field. He sat on the earth, wringing out his coat, sheltered from the wind by the tall stalks of grain, and when he had rested a little, he listened for the sound of voices and stood up.

Walking slowly along the edge of the field, he saw a hayrack moving down a road that ran past a farmhouse. As he chafed his arms to warm himself, the morning mist in the distance began to clear, and by the time he had reached the road he could see that he was coming toward a city. Webb dropped the compass into a drainage ditch, threw the rucksack into the field, and dried his pistol as he walked.

The morning breeze blew across the fields, chilling him momentarily, and he turned up the collar of his coat, as though its wet mass would shield him from the cold. Watching the spires of the city ahead, he forced himself to walk faster, for the day had almost begun, and he had to reach the little shop on Michalska Street before sunrise.

As he came into the town, his tired mind dredged for memories that would help him, tried to visualize a plan of Bratislava, but nothing concrete would detach itself from his leaden brain and he blundered ahead, afraid to ask the vegetable woman or the milkman pausing beside his dog cart.

Ahead of him Webb saw a policeman trudging toward his post, and he slowed so that he would not overtake him. A few blocks more, and Webb passed the gates of a factory changing shifts. The moving crowd gave him a brief sense of companionship as men and women jostled against him on their way home. Keeping his eyes toward the sidewalk, he walked only a few feet behind a cluster of apathetic factory workers, trying to blend with them each time he crossed intersections where he was naked to scrutiny from four directions.

The street signs were meaningless to him, and he was guided only by his sense of direction and a decision to follow streetcar tracks into the center of town. As he moved away from the outskirts, he saw more policemen, fishmongers, delivery boys on bicycles; heard the occasional grinding of a streetcar in the distance. His throat went dry each time someone seemed to look at him, and his breath quickened until he could feel his heart pounding. Then there would be moments when he could see no one at all, and his throat would moisten and his breathing would slow to normal. A streetcar clanged past at an intersection, and Webb read the sign on it: Komensky, the name of Bratislava's university.

The pavement under his feet was smooth and worn, the curbs well defined. With every passing block the buildings were taller, the shop windows better trimmed. A workman passed him, riding a bicycle, and Webb could smell the steam of hot coffee drifting from his lunch pail. His throat tightened with wanting, and then the sweet, dimly remembered smell was gone.

Another streetcar ground past, and as he read its destination automatically, the word Michalska stood out as though it were formed in fluorescent light. He wanted to run after the streetcar, shout at the motorman to stop, board it, and slump into a seat while he was carried effortlessly to his goal. Because he had no idea of how one boarded a streetcar in Bratislava, the price of a ride, or whether a special pass was required. Webb set his teeth and watched the streetcar until it turned three blocks ahead.

In fifteen minutes he saw what he felt must be St. Michael's Gate, standing solidly astride Michalska Street. His eyes searched the shop windows near the gate, trying to decipher the unfamiliar word combinations, the strangely accented Czech letters.

As Karel had told him, the last shop, the one against St. Michael's Gate, was lettered in gold leaf with the word Domace. His eyes smarted at the sight and he rubbed them with a dirty sleeve. None of the shops were open, and the only sign of life between him and the gate was an old man pasting a picture poster of President Gottwald against a wall. Webb looked into each shop window for a moment as he moved near the gate, killing time until the old man would leave. When he finally saw him shuffle away with his brush, glue pot, and stack of posters, Webb looked into the front window of Domace, and rang the bell at the door.

The little chimes rang through the clear morning air like breaking crystal, chilling him with the thought that their sound would bring the police. He tried to define the dark outlines inside the window, but the shop was dark.

Webb rang again.

This time the chimes did not rasp his drawn nerves, and he peered intently inside the shop, forgetting that any casual passer could see him. The seconds crawled until Webb saw a stab of gray inside the shop. Slippered feet crossed the floor inside, and he heard the bolt being drawn. The door opened, snubbed by a chain, and an old woman looked down at him. She said something Webb did not understand, and Webb leaned against the frame of the door and said, "Herta Sebok."

The door closed instantly.

Webb did not wait to hear her slippered feet shuffling away. He pounded on the door and rang the chimes again. Through the window he could see the old woman huddled in her blue shawl and nightgown, staring at the door, then at his face looking up at her. Webb pounded again, cursing her softly, and finally the door opened again. This time the snub chain was not in sight, and Webb pushed the door open roughly and stepped into the shop. He closed the door with the chain, shot the bolt, and said, "I've got to see Herta Sebok."

The old woman shrugged her shoulders, turned from him, and shuffled toward a curtain-hung doorway at the back of the shop.

Webb followed her around glass display cases filled with stamps and greeting cards, into a living room, bedroom, and kitchen in one small room. The old woman knelt in front of the iron stove, struck a match, and lighted a wood fire under the grate, ignoring him.

Webb said, "I've come a long way to see Herta. Will you tell her Kaspar is here?"

The old woman closed the door, got slowly to her feet and said, in fair English, "Where you know Herta?"

"In Prague."

"When?"

"Last week." His knees were turning to liquid from fatigue. He leaned against the bed-couch for support.

The old woman's face was a gray plaster mask. "You knew her friends?"

Webb nodded. "Czarny, Eduard, and Karlo."

The woman's eyes flickered. "You were to meet them here?"

"No."

"Why not?"

"Because they're dead," Webb said, in sorrow and anger. "They were killed at Ruzyne, helping me get away."

"Then why you come back?"

"Ask Herta," Webb said. He sat down on the bed, put his hands over his face, and rested his elbows on his knees. His body was a network of crippling pain. He did not want to think any more, or argue with the old woman. His mind was almost past caring. If he had found his way into a trap, he knew it was the end; and because that would mean that Karel had been caught, he knew that he would not want to live.

The old woman said, "You are tired, Kaspar?"

Webb parted his fingers and looked at her. "I feel fine," he said bitterly. "I've walked here from Vienna, stumbled through a forest at night, killed two men, and rowed across the Danube in a leaky skiff." He looked at his hands, his torn clothing, his mud-caked shoes. "If you've never heard of Herta Sebok, that's fine, too. Just give me a pot of tea, let me sleep here a few hours, and I'll go away."

The old woman nodded, drew water into a pot, and began polishing a heavy crockery mug with a corner of her shawl. When she had put the water over the fire, she came to Webb, knelt down, and pulled off his shoes. He watched her wrap the shoes in newspaper and stuff them into a trash barrel. Then he lay back and closed his eyes.

When he woke, the room was dark and the fire had gone out. Someone sat beside the couch, and at first his eyes saw only the outline of the old woman. He asked, "What time is it?"

"Nearly noon," the old woman said. She got up from her stool and brought back a teapot and crockery mug.

Webb drank deeply, coughing a little between gulps, and when he had finished, he said, "Did you tell her?"

The old woman took away the mug and the teapot. "I told her."

"Is she coming?"

"She is coming," the old woman said.

"When?"

The old woman began washing the teapot. "Tonight, perhaps." She shrugged her shoulders. "Perhaps tomorrow. As soon as it is safe."

"Did she have a message for me?"

The old woman held up the crockery mug and dried it with a corner of her shawl. "She said that she loves you, and that you are to wait here until she comes. She said that you must be ready to leave at once, as soon as she gets here."

Webb's throat went tight, and he could not tell whether it was from relief or from fear. "Did she say that I was to leave alone, or—"

The old woman looked at him with scorn, and then she smiled. "If you were to leave alone, for what reason would she ask you to wait for her?"

She opened a cupboard and put away the teapot and the crockery mug. She said, "You will wait for her?"

Webb closed his eyes, feeling sleep come over him that even the pounding of his heart could not put off. "Yes," he said, to the dark room. "I'll wait."

THE END

Manufactured by Amazon.ca
Bolton, ON

20570401R00111